"I feel that we understand each other. I feel that we're friends. And maybe you don't feel the same way, but—"

"I feel the same way." The words were out of his mouth before he could help it.

Her breath gave a funny little hitch. "Maybe it isn't rare, this feeling." She gestured between them. "Maybe it's just that I haven't found it with anyone else because I've been indulging in my grief for too long. But I don't have to pretend anything with you and it feels..."

"It feels?"

She shrugged, her eyes a little wild. "Like heaven," she hiccupped.

Which was exactly how he felt knowing she didn't care one jot about his scars.

He didn't know if he'd moved first or if she had, but their lips met with a firm warmth that was neither rushed nor urgent, but irresistible for all that.

Dear Reader,

Chloe and Beau's story had been circling in my mind for some time. I knew I wanted to write a "Beauty and the Beast"-type story with a scarred hero. But as my hero Beau turned to his beautiful but neglected walled garden for solace, elements of *A Secret Garden* started to creep in too. Enter my garden designer heroine to help him make over said garden and turn his dream into a reality. When my editor suggested I write it as a Christmas story, everything finally fell into place and I couldn't wait to start writing it.

I love Christmas romances. I think they have an extra dash of sparkle—maybe it's the tinsel and the lights—but I actually think things like family and belonging matter a whole lot more at Christmas. At Christmastime, it really feels as if wishes and dreams can come true.

Chloe has lost her Christmas mojo, while Beau has lost his zest for life. In making over Beau's beautiful garden, however, hearts and spirits heal. And along the way these two come to realise the true meaning of Christmas.

Wishing you all a holiday season filled with much love, laughter and joy!

Big hugs,

Michelle

Reclusive Millionaire's Mistletoe Miracle

—

Michelle Douglas

HARLEQUIN

Romance

HARLEQUIN®

Romance™

Recycling programs
for this product may
not exist in your area.

ISBN-13: 978-1-335-73685-7

Reclusive Millionaire's Mistletoe Miracle

Harlequin Enterprises ULC
22 Adelaide St. West, 41st Floor
Toronto, Ontario M5H 4E3, Canada
www.Harlequin.com

Printed in U.S.A.

Michelle Douglas has been writing for Harlequin since 2007 and believes she has the best job in the world. She lives in a leafy suburb of Newcastle, on Australia's east coast, with her own romantic hero, a house full of dust and books, and an eclectic collection of '60s and '70s vinyl. She loves to hear from readers and can be contacted via her website, michelle-douglas.com.

Books by Michelle Douglas

Harlequin Romance

The Million Pound Marriage Deal
Miss Prim's Greek Island Fling
The Maid, the Millionaire and the Baby
Redemption of the Maverick Millionaire
Singapore Fling with the Millionaire
Secret Billionaire on Her Doorstep
Billionaire's Road Trip to Forever
Cinderella and the Brooding Billionaire
Escape with Her Greek Tycoon
Wedding Date in Malaysia

Visit the Author Profile page
at Harlequin.com for more titles.

To Sue, for raising two fabulous children and putting up with this crazy family with humor and grace.

Praise for
Michelle Douglas

CHAPTER ONE

CHLOE SWORE AS she slipped and skidded across the cobblestoned courtyard from the converted coach house to the back door of the big house, the heavy dew making the trip perilous. Her feet started to slide out from beneath her and she windmilled her arms wildly, catching hold of the door handle at the last moment. She held on for grim life until she was sure she'd regained her balance, and then pounded on the door with more vigour than grace, muttering a slew of equally inelegant curses under her breath.

Welcome to Devon, Chlo.

Pulling her coat around her, she tried jogging on the spot, her breath frosting the air, as she tried to prevent the cold from creeping into her very bones. It was *freezing*! And it wasn't even December yet. How was it possible to be this cold?

She knocked again—though it was more of a beating of her fists as her extremities started to lose all feeling—and then fumbled in her pocket for her phone and hit redial. She'd had to ring the number of the big house earlier after she'd got so lost from the directions the locals had given her that she'd become convinced that the people who lived in this part of the world had no sense of direction *at all*.

Deep inside the house she heard the phone ringing, just as the back door opened.

She tried to turn her phone off, but her hands were shaking too hard.

'Chloe, what happened to you? You're soaked!' Stephanie Gladstone, the housekeeper she'd met briefly earlier this evening, pulled her inside and closed the door, before taking her phone and turning it off. 'Come with me, quickly! We need to get you warm.'

Yes, please.

In next to no time, she found herself sitting in front of a heater in the kitchen, her hair up in a towel, and her wet things removed in favour of a thick fluffy robe that Stephanie had seemed to magic out of the air. She accepted the mug of steaming cocoa Stephanie held out to her, with a grateful, 'Thank you.'

She blew on it, the steam lifting to warm her face, and momentarily closed her eyes to savour that very first sip. She touched the mug to her lips, eager for that first hit of hot sweetness, but before she could take a sip a large wolf of a man stormed into the kitchen with the kind of ferocious scowl that in ordinary circumstances might make her quail. But not today.

'What in the name of God is all this infernal racket?'

He bristled all over, the rangy frame crackling with energy and outrage and temper.

His gaze zeroed in on her and his brows lowered even further over his eyes. 'And who the hell are you?'

She recognised him immediately. Setting her mug down, she shot to her feet. 'I'm Chloe Ivy Belle Jennings, and if this is the way you usually speak to your employees, Mr Beau Diamond, you can shove your contract where the sun doesn't shine and find somebody else to be your damn lackey.'

She wasn't sure why she used her full name, only it did sound more impressive. *And* it made him blink. At least, she thought that was what made him blink.

To her right, Stephanie huffed out a laugh. 'That'll tell you, Beau. Stop bellyaching. A water pipe in the flat has burst. I've got George onto it, but you're going to need to get the plumbers back.'

'And probably someone to fix the soggy wall. And the carpet will be ruined as well,' Chloe added for good measure. Water had gone everywhere at a ridiculous rate of knots.

He swung back. 'Why on earth didn't you turn the water off at the mains?'

He stared at her as if she were stupid and she didn't bother trying to put a lid on her temper. Today had been trying on so many levels and this was one straw too many. 'If I could've found the mains, I would've! If we're asking searching questions, why the hell did you give me such substandard accommodation?'

Accommodation had been part of the contract. She didn't require much, but warm and dry were non-negotiable.

She'd been told before that she had ferocious eyebrows and she did what she could to use them to best effect now, frowning as fiercely as she could. But then she realised what a sight she must look, in this enormous fluffy robe and her hair wrapped in a towel, and had to fight an insane urge to laugh.

Not funny share-a-joke laughter, but the kind that held a hint of hysteria. Turning her back on the grump of a man, she lifted the cocoa to her lips and took a big sustaining gulp, closing her eyes and feeling it warm her all the way through.

'Well, you can't stay here.'

She swung around. 'If you think I'm leaving in the dead of night to find accommodation in the village then you're going to be rudely disappointed, Mr Diamond.'

His eyes widened as she advanced on him. At the back of her mind she noted his rumpled appearance and the too-long hair that was sticking up all over the place as if he'd just jumped out of bed. Which, of course, was exactly what he had done. But at least he hadn't had to slosh through icy water!

She stopped in front of him. 'Do you know how long it took me to get from my door to yours?'

He shook his head, eyeing her as if she were some rogue wildebeest from the plains of Africa.

'It was thirty-four hours from the time I left my house in Sydney to when I stepped off the plane at Heathrow. It took an hour on the Tube to get to Paddington train station and then it was a four-hour train journey to Barnstaple. At that point there was a problem with my hire car booking, which delayed me for the best part of an hour, but then according to my satnav it was supposed to be a simple seventeen-minute Sunday drive to the apparently idyllic but tiny village of Ballingsmallard and a further two minutes to Dawncarden Court.'

He cleared his throat and nodded. 'That's correct.'

'Hallelujah, I said to myself.' The words left her on a growl. 'But the satnav was wrong!' She shook her head so hard the towel on her head unravelled and her wild mane of hair fell down below her shoulders, which probably made her look more and more like that rogue wildebeest by the minute. It wasn't an image that improved her temper.

She stabbed a finger at him. 'The people in this part of the world clearly don't know their left from their right or...or which way is even up! So I wasn't sent on just one, but *three* wild goose chases. Nobody warned me that I'd lose satellite signal, so I didn't bother printing a map out. Why didn't *you* warn me?'

He adjusted his stance. 'How long did it take for you to find Dawncarden Court?'

'Three hours eighteen minutes and thirty-three seconds!'

He winced and glanced at Stephanie. 'I thought you'd—'

'And I thought you had.'

She ignored them. 'And now I don't know whether I'm coming or going! I'm jet-lagged, tired, cold, wet and hungry. And if you think I'm going back out there—' she pointed in the vague direction of the road outside '—to try and find a room at the inn, then you're more wrong than you have ever been.'

They eyed each other across what seemed like some invisible divide, and to her amazement he eventually shrugged. 'Well, I'm sure we can at least do something about you being hungry, can't we, Steph?'

'Already on it,' Stephanie said, cracking eggs into a frying pan.

Chloe stared and her entire frame drooped. 'Oh, but I didn't mean to put you to any trouble.' She moistened her lips, fighting a wave of exhaustion. 'I just wanted to get warm and dry and...'

'And to have a rest,' the older woman finished for her, 'and that's entirely understandable. Sit down and finish your cocoa. I'll have this whipped up in no time and you'll feel all the better for it, I promise. Would you like some as well, Beau?'

'Why not?' With a shrug he hooked out a chair at right angles to Chloe. She buried her nose in her mug, and squinted slightly to blur his outline, tried not to wince. Had she really just ranted at her employer like a fishwife?

Holding the mug in both hands, she stared into its contents. 'I think I probably owe you an apology for, um…going off like a firecracker just now.'

'Not at all.'

She didn't believe him. In her mind, she replayed what she'd just said and heat flooded her face. She stared all the more doggedly into her mug. 'Tomorrow, when my brain is hopefully in decent working order again, I'll try and apologise properly and…' Try and find a way to prove to him that normally she had the most level of tempers.

'You are allowed to look at me when you speak,' he snapped.

She did what she could to smother the yawn that threatened to split her face in two as she turned towards him. 'What?'

'I won't bite.'

But his voice had lost its venom and a furrow appeared between his eyes. She huffed out a laugh, too tired to try and work out what any of it meant…too tired to even care if she'd still have a job in the morning.

Don't be daft. You need this job.

'So you're saying your bark is worse than your bite, then?'

'I'm glad to see you've got his number.' Stephanie set plates of scrambled eggs and toast in front of them. 'Stop pestering the poor girl, Beau, and let her eat. She's too tired for your nonsense.'

She decided then and there that she loved Stephanie.

'Where were you thinking of putting Ms Jennings, Steph?'

'Chloe,' Chloe said around a mouthful of egg. 'Please call me Chloe. Ms Jennings is my mum.' She gestured to her plate with her fork. 'These are the best scrambled eggs ever.'

'In the daffodil room.'

'But—'

'Oh, that sounds lovely,' Chloe murmured, finding it a sudden effort to chew and swallow...to even lift her fork. Now that she felt deliciously warm again, she wasn't sure she ever wanted to move. 'Daffodils are the happiest flowers, don't you think? So warm and yellow and everything. Daffodils and wattle and sunflowers and Billy buttons...'

'Oops, we're losing her,' she heard Steph say at the same time as a warm strong hand wrapped around her upper arm.

She jerked back into immediate wakefulness. Even through the thickness of the towelling robe, she could feel the unmistakable strength of Beau Diamond's fingers and it made something weird stir to life inside her.

She jerked upright. 'Sorry!'

'No problem.' He removed his hand.

'I don't know what's wrong with me. I feel drunk. But I've not had any alcohol since...' She shook her head. She wasn't a drinker. 'It'd be weeks.' Maybe months. 'And my balance is off.'

'That'll be due to the air travel. The balance thing,' he clarified. 'As for the rest, Chloe, basically you've been travelling for two days with very little sleep and probably not a whole lot of food either. You need to finish your eggs.'

He gestured at her plate, so she forked more egg into her mouth and then ate half a slice of toast for good measure.

'And you need to keep hydrated.'

He poured her a glass of water and she drank it—greedily. She hadn't even realised she was thirsty.

'And now you need to sleep and sleep until you don't feel like sleeping any more.'

How divine that sounded. 'Don't we have a meeting tomorrow?'

He reached out a hand to prop her up when she started to list again. 'The day after. Tomorrow you rest.'

She made a half-hearted effort to straighten up again. But it was kind of nice to feel that firm strength—all warm and reassuring through the towelling robe. So it was only half an effort. She found a smile. 'Do you know how good that sounds?'

One side of his mouth hooked up. 'I've got some idea.'

For a fraction of a moment something in his eyes danced and a sigh fluttered out of her. 'You have the loveliest eyes.' They were the colour of a deep blue sea. 'I never noticed that from the telly.'

His smile vanished and she forced herself to straighten. 'While I apparently, or so I am told, have fierce eyebrows.'

He blinked.

'And I do believe they stopped you barking at me earlier, so I'm rather grateful to them.'

She found herself frowning. 'And why are the two of you letting me rattle on with nonsense like this?'

Stephanie laughed. 'Because it's refreshingly direct and I like it. But you're right. It's time you were in bed. Come along and I'll show you your room.'

Grateful, she pushed to her feet. 'Goodnight, Beau. I can call you Beau, can't I? Or do we have to do the awful formal Mr Diamond and Ms Jennings thing?'

'Beau will be fine.'

With a salute, she turned and followed Stephanie from the room. 'I think I'm going to die a thousand deaths when I remember all of this to-morrow,' she whispered.

'Nonsense.' Stephanie laughed. 'You're exactly what the doctor ordered and I can't tell you how glad I am to welcome you to Dawncarden Court, Chloe.'

Chloe crossed her fingers as hard as she could and hoped that Beau Diamond was nowhere to be seen before stepping into the kitchen the next morning. She gave an audible sigh before leaping across to fill the kettle.

Coffee. Please. Now.

'Good morning, Chloe.'

She whirled around with a yelp when a deep voice sounded behind her. 'Oh, Lord! Lordy lord. You just took ten years off my life.' She patted her chest and tried to find a smile. 'Good morning... Beau.'

One rather commanding eyebrow rose. 'Were you just *tiptoeing* through my house?'

'You bet your sweet patootie I was. I figured I'd disturbed you enough last night. I wanted to prove I could be as quiet as the proverbial mouse when occasion demanded it.'

He didn't laugh. He didn't even smile.

She swallowed. 'Is it okay to grab a cuppa before I head into the village to find alternative lodgings?'

He might have an enormous house, but it was

clear he didn't want to share it. And as someone who valued her privacy too—though coming from as big a family as she did, privacy was a relative term—she didn't blame him.

'Help yourself to a decent breakfast. It'll help your body clock adjust.'

'Thank you. Coffee?'

He shook his head, but he didn't leave. He just stood there and watched her.

In the cold light of morning—*late* morning and, yes, it did look cold—last night's impression of height and breadth hadn't been misleading, and the energy he'd once projected onto the television screen from his natural history documentary series was still present, but any humour she might've once imagined in that face had well and truly disappeared. Unfortunately she hadn't dreamed that bristling, brooding undercurrent thing that he had going either.

Swallowing a sigh, she made a coffee and eased into a seat at the table. 'Do I still have a job?'

He moved across to the kitchen bench. 'Yes.'

She closed her eyes. *Thank you. Thank you. Thank you.*

Winning the contract to make over Dawncarden Court's walled garden had been a lifesaver, and about the only thing standing between her and losing the house she and Mark had saved so hard for. She'd put so much work into her submission. Had brushed up on all things associated with English country gardens until her brain had been in danger of exploding. She'd wanted to wow him with her knowledge of the local climate, of local plants and soil types, of English native trees. And it had paid off.

Don't mess it up.

Forcing her eyes open, she sipped her coffee and glanced back up at him. Even though it was a good twelve months since he'd been on TV, she'd have still recognised him. Even given the accident and his scars, and she wasn't sure why, but that felt like a relief. 'Would you like me to attempt a proper apology now or—?'

'I'd really rather you didn't.'

He didn't turn back, and she craned her neck to see what he was doing. Oh, he was making tea! Why hadn't she asked him if he wanted tea? 'Well, for what it's worth, I *am* sorry. I'm not usually so bad-tempered.'

'Jet lag.' He set a large teapot to the middle of the table along with two mugs before lowering that tall rangy frame to the seat opposite. Despite the mellowness of his tone, when he glanced at her the blue of his eyes was oddly piercing. 'How are you feeling today?'

She gulped more coffee. 'Like I'm hung over, but without the headache. You've been a globe-trotter, what are your tips and tricks for overcoming jet lag?'

* * *

Before he could answer, Stephanie came tripping into the kitchen. She'd been dealing with the plumbers she'd called first thing to look at the burst pipes in the flat.

'You need to start eating your meals in this time zone, rather than when you feel hungry, as well as drinking lots of water, and getting out in the sun for a walk,' she said with her usual crispness.

Chloe choked on her coffee. 'Sun?' She pointed towards the window. 'You're calling that weak excuse for a bit of light the sun?'

He found himself wanting to laugh. Just as he'd wanted to laugh several times last night. But just as he had last night, he suppressed the urge. He didn't trust it. 'Getting out into the daylight will help your body clock reset itself.'

She stared at him, dragged in a breath and then nodded. 'Okay, but... I had no idea how cold it'd be here.'

He and Stephanie exchanged glances but didn't inform her that there was nothing particularly cold about the current weather. She'd flown in from an Australian summer to an English winter. It'd take her a few days to acclimatise.

'Once you're properly rested, the cold won't seem so bad,' he found himself assuring her.

Stephanie glanced at him with a raised eyebrow, but he studiously ignored it, pouring them mugs of tea instead. Thankfully, she fetched the cake tin and cut them all a generous slice of Madeira cake.

'Oh, but…' Chloe started.

'Eat,' Stephanie ordered. 'I have a proposition for you both and the cake will help sweeten it.'

His gut instantly clenched. He knew immediately what this proposition of Stephanie's was. She was going to suggest that Chloe *Ivy Belle* Jennings stay here in the manor for the duration of her contract, and while he knew it made sense everything inside him protested. He'd rather the expense of having to put her up in the village.

Damn it! It was *his* house. *He* made the rules.

Stephanie fixed him with an eagle eye as if she'd read that thought in his face. She didn't challenge him, though, didn't say it wasn't his house yet and that it was his grandmother who made the rules. Not for the first time he could see why his grandmother had engaged her as housekeeper twenty years ago. He expected the two women would see eye to eye on most things.

From the corner of his eye, he saw Chloe take a bite of cake and a momentary expression of bliss crossed her face—as if she hadn't eaten cake in a long time and had forgotten how good it could be. She captured a crumb at the corner of her mouth with her tongue and things low down in his belly suddenly clenched, taking him off guard.

What the hell…?

Scowling, he took a huge bite of cake. All he

could say was that he was glad her ridiculous hair was pulled back in a thick plait this morning. When the towel had worked its way loose from her hair last night and all of that gingerbread-coloured hair had tumbled halfway down her back, he'd not been able to do anything for a moment but stare.

His scowl deepened. It was ridiculous hair for a gardener to have!

'You can get that expression off your face right now, Beau Diamond,' Stephanie told him in no uncertain terms. 'And you *will* hear me out.'

'As I've yet to find a way to stop you from speaking your mind,' he returned just as swiftly, 'then I expect you're right.'

That made her laugh. Very little disturbed Stephanie's equanimity.

'What did the tradesmen say?'

'The plumbing is old—that renovation was done back in the sixties. To be on the safe side, they want to replace all the pipes. According to George, it's just as well someone was staying at the time as that pipe could've gone at any moment.'

Stephanie turned to Chloe. 'George is our general handyman. When he's not busy mending fences and replacing tiles in the rooves of the various outbuildings, he cuts the grass, keeps the vegetable patch in order, and prunes what he can, but the gardens here are too much for one person.

He lives in the village, but I'll introduce the two of you later.'

Chloe nodded and went back to her cake.

Stephanie swung back to Beau. 'Because it was found early the water damage isn't too extensive. But I expect some painting and new carpet will be necessary.'

He sighed. It wasn't the expense that bothered him—there was plenty of money for repairs—but the thought of tradesmen in and out of Dawncarden had his hands clenching.

Well, Stephanie could deal with them. It was one of the things he paid her for after all.

'I spoke to Julia last night.'

Hearing the concern in her voice, he set his mug down.

'Julia is my daughter,' she explained to Chloe. 'And she's pregnant.'

'That's lovely news. Congratulations.'

He didn't want to like Chloe Jennings. He didn't want to have any feelings for her whatsoever. But he couldn't deny that she had a nice smile. And when she wasn't in a temper, her eyebrows didn't look the least bit fierce.

He shook himself. 'Is everything okay?'

'The morning sickness hasn't passed and she's sounding tired…a little glum.'

'But she and the baby…?'

'They're both fine. But I'm worried about her,

Beau. She wants me to spend Christmas with them.'

But Julia lived in Newcastle! That was a six-and-a-half-hour drive away. It wasn't exactly a hop, skip and jump to go and have Christmas dinner with her daughter and then get back to Dawn-carden Court to cook his supper.

Not that he needed her to cook his supper. He knew his way around a kitchen. But—

'I want to take some leave, some proper leave. I've not had a holiday in years. I've not spent more than a weekend away from the estate in two years.' She folded her arms. 'I've earned some time off.'

He wanted to argue, but she was right. He couldn't begrudge her the time off. Especially if she was worried about Julia. And it *was* coming up to Christmas. Not that he gave two hoots about the season for himself, but it seemed to mean a lot to other people.

None of that stopped a scowl from settling over his features, though.

'Don't look at me like that,' she ordered, clearly not the least put out. 'I've come up with the perfect solution.'

It was his turn to cross his arms. Across the table he was aware of Chloe's gaze on his arms. His lips twisted. Checking them for scars no doubt. The entire world was hungry for news—and photographs—of his scars.

He forced his focus back to Stephanie. 'The

perfect solution?' He suspected that as far as he was going to be concerned it would be far from perfect.

'If Chloe here is amenable, she could fill in as temporary housekeeper for a few weeks.'

Chloe straightened. 'Oh, I...'

She swallowed and he sympathised. Stephanie could be hard to withstand.

'What would it entail?'

'Not a lot. Cooking the evening meal and a little light cleaning. We have a house-cleaning service that comes in once a week to do a comprehensive spit and polish, but they're banned from Beau's rooms, so whipping through those areas with a duster and giving them a quick vacuum is about all you'll be asked to do. The supermarket in the village will deliver whatever you need...and—'

'And nothing,' Beau cut in. 'I can deal with all of that myself. I know how to cook and clean as well as the next person.'

Steph raised an eyebrow. 'And are you also prepared to deal with the tradesmen and the house-cleaning service?'

Hell, no.

'I thought not,' she said, evidently reading the answer in his face. 'And before you suggest it, you're not cancelling either. This is your grandmother's estate, and, while you'll inherit it one day, she's my employer and this is the kind of property that can get away from a body if they let it. I'm following her instructions, not yours.'

Damn it!

'How long are you planning to be away?' he demanded.

'Until after the new year.'

'But that's *six weeks*!'

'I've earned it, Beau. And I need a break.'

He dragged a hand down his face. Across the table, Chloe watched them with eyes the colour of treacle.

Steph gestured towards her. 'You saw Chloe in action last night. She's not the kind of girl tradesmen *or* the press will be able to walk over.'

He glared at Stephanie, wanting to bellow at her that she wasn't allowed to go anywhere. But he didn't have the right. And he couldn't begrudge her time away with her family.

'If neither of you like that idea, then I can organise a temporary housekeeper from a reputable agency.'

'That is *not* going to happen.'

He wasn't having yet another person in his space. Strangers couldn't be trusted. That had already been established.

This Chloe Jennings probably couldn't be trusted either, but her garden design had been the best, and her knowledge of the local flora and ecosystems had impressed him. And he *had* made her sign a watertight privacy clause. If she tried to leak photographs of him to the tabloids, he'd sue her for every penny she had and utterly destroy her professional reputation while he was at it.

'Are you seeing sense yet, Beau?'

'Chloe hasn't agreed to the arrangement, Steph, and I don't see why she'd want to.'

'Of course she will, won't you, Chloe? For one thing, you'll receive a generous stipend on top of what you're already being paid for the garden makeover.'

Chloe's eyes brightened, and things inside him hardened. Was he going to need to lock the family silver up while she was here?

'I don't have any objections to the plan.' Chloe glanced at him uncertainly. 'I'm a passable cook and can certainly cope with a bit of light cleaning, but you don't seem the least bit keen. And as my gardening contract comes first…'

Stephanie spread her hands. 'So can I go and pack my bags yet, or do I need to call the agency?'

He bit back an oath and swung to Chloe, knowing his face had turned ferocious, probably scary, and certainly ugly. It was what he saw whenever he looked in the mirror these days—ugly, jagged scars. To her credit, she barely blinked. But that was probably because she was still jet-lagged.

'I want us very clear on one thing.' He stabbed a finger to the table so hard it jolted his entire arm. It took a force of will not to wince.

Serves you right for trying to be a tough dude.

'That privacy clause you signed in relation to the garden will also extend to this temporary housekeeping gig too. Do I make myself clear?'

'Perfectly.'

'And I'll be making you sign a document to that effect.'

'Okay.' She glanced at Stephanie. 'Privacy is a big deal around here, then?'

'Absolutely.' Stephanie started clearing the table. 'His lordship here has a real bee in his bonnet about it. If it were up to him, he'd never leave this place and would refuse to see anyone. Hence the reason you'll need to be the one to deal with the tradesmen and anyone else who might come knocking on the door.'

'Does anyone come knocking?'

'Not so much any more, but we do still get the occasional journalist looking for a story and hoping to catch a glimpse of Beau.'

Those not so ferocious eyebrows shot up.

'Apparently the price of an up-to-date picture of Beau is now rumoured to be upward of the twenty-thousand-pound mark.'

Chloe shot forward on her seat. 'You have to be joking! That's…it's—'

'Hence the privacy clause I insisted you sign.'

She slumped back and his every instinct went on high alert. Given a chance, would this girl try and sell him out?

'And if you break that clause, I will sue you for

every dollar you have and more, do I make myself clear?'

Her eyes widened, and then those brows did become ferocious. 'I've no intention of breaking my contract with you, *Mr Diamond*, but if you're worried that I might, then you're free to make other arrangements for your housekeeper and I'll find accommodation in the village. I'm more than happy to speak to the housekeeper about the garden rather than you.'

That certainly wasn't going to happen. The garden was too precious to him. Too *necessary*.

He shook his head. 'The more I think about it, the more Stephanie's plan makes sense. It also makes sense to have you right here where I can keep an eye on you, rather than staying in the village where you might be tempted to gossip. The fewer people working at Dawncarden, the better, and the less the likelihood of the press getting a picture of me.'

Stephanie clapped briskly. 'Excellent! The lord and master has spoken.'

Chloe drooped in her chair like a flower in dire need of water and he winced. He'd become a bad-tempered beast since the accident, but he hadn't wanted her misunderstanding the gravity of that privacy clause.

You all but accused her of wanting to sell pictures of you to the press.

No, he hadn't! He'd just made it plain where they stood.

She shook her head. 'And yet you don't look happy about the arrangement.'

'Since the accident that's been his permanent expression,' Stephanie said. 'If he's not careful, the wind will change and he'll be stuck with a face like thunder forever.'

Given his scars, what did it matter? 'When did you say you were leaving?' he growled.

Chloe gurgled out a laugh. 'I'm going to miss this sniping. Is that part of the job description?'

'Absolutely,' Stephanie said.

At the same time as he said, 'Don't even think about it.'

But some of the blackness of his mood lifted.

'Are you really a lord?' Chloe asked.

'No, that's simply what passes as a joke to Stephanie.'

'I like her sense of humour.'

So did he but he wouldn't admit it, not even under threat of torture.

'If it's any consolation, the remuneration package will be very generous,' he found himself saying.

'Consolation for what—your bad temper?' She stood. 'I guess time will tell. If today is my last day of leisure, then I'm going for that walk and praying you're right about it helping me beat the jet lag blues.'

When she'd gone, Stephanie swung to him. 'If you ever spoke to me the way you just spoke to that young woman, I'd resign on the spot. She doesn't deserve your nasty suspicions or your rudeness. You're turning into a bitter, bad-tempered man, Beau, and you need to do something about that.'

'Why?'

'Because this is no way to live! You shut yourself away here and what good is it doing you? You're letting your talent go to waste—'

'The world no longer wants my talent!'

Soon, though, he'd have his garden and perhaps his world wouldn't look quite so bleak. Maybe then he'd find the resources to manage a semblance of politeness and civility.

CHAPTER TWO

'OH, MY GOD! You ought to see Dawncarden Court, Mum. It's amazing!' Chloe gushed before her mother could start fussing and worrying again about Chloe not spending Christmas at home.

This year she was determined to not wreck her family's Christmas. She'd been the kiss of death to the last two and that was more than enough. This year her family deserved to celebrate the season with joy and laughter. She was determined to give them *nothing* to worry about.

She had promised to video-call regularly while in England, though. She was hoping it'd be easier to fake Christmas cheer from ten thousand miles away than it would be if she were still in Australia. In her lap she crossed her fingers.

Her mother's face moved closer to the screen as if she was trying to peer into her daughter's soul. 'You're not brooding, are you, love? You know it's time to move on and—'

'Absolutely not! This is all such an adventure. I'm planning on enjoying every moment of it. And seriously, when I show you pictures of this place, you're going to see exactly what I mean.'

She did her best to describe the house and gardens. Not that she'd yet seen the walled garden. Oh, she'd found it—the wall at least. That had been impossible to miss. But the door had been locked. When she'd mentioned it to Stephanie, the other woman had shown her the hook behind the door where the key was hung. 'Next time I call, I'll do it from the baronial hall so you can see it. It'll knock your—'

She blinked when a large hand reached across and snapped her laptop shut. Glancing up, she found Beau straightening from the other side of the table. 'What—?'

She choked back the rest of her words at the expression on his face. He looked as if he wanted to throttle her, and it suddenly occurred to her that she was alone with a man who, for all she knew, could be a Bluebeard in his castle. Why hadn't she asked Stephanie more about him?

She should've asked for a character reference or something. At least an assurance that the man was in his right mind. Her heart thudded. She'd so badly needed the contract she'd been more focussed on proving her own credentials than checking his.

'Already selling me out, Ms Jennings?'

She frowned. Hold on, he thought…?

'What is wrong with you?' she found herself shouting. He'd cut off her call to her mother because he'd thought she was talking to someone from the press? *Seriously?*

And seriously, had she just *shouted*? She never shouted.

Thrusting out her jaw, she glared. Beau Diamond's nasty suspicions deserved to be yelled at. Besides, her rations of 'nice and polite' had been severely depleted prior to arriving here—burned out, in fact, hence the need for the strategic retreat from her family. Now that she'd relaxed her guard she was finding it impossible to get even a semblance of 'nice and polite' back into place.

She tipped what was left of her now tepid coffee into the sink. Was she going to have to put up with this mentality for the next two months? 'Have you thought about therapy? Because you're starting to sound ridiculously paranoid.'

His jaw dropped. '*Paranoid?* You were giving detailed descriptions of the lie of the land so a photographer would know the best vantage points to lie in wait and hopefully get a picture of me. *And* you were promising pictures of the inside of the house! There's nothing paranoid about that. You can pack your damn bags and—'

'You *idiot*! I was talking to my *mum*, not some sleazy journalist. God! When are you going to get it into your thick skull that I'm not interested in selling you out?'

They stared at each other, both breathing hard. Beau eventually swallowed and rolled his shoulders. 'Your mum?'

'My mum,' she repeated, flipping open the lid of her laptop.

He didn't move, not a single muscle.

'And now you're going to meet her.'

That galvanised him again. 'I don't *do* face-to-face interviews with *anyone*.'

She curled her lip in his general direction. It seemed better than calling him a rude name. 'This isn't an interview.' She planted herself in her chair in front of her computer again and punched a few keys.

'I'm not—'

'If you don't, I'm leaving.' She leaned back and folded her arms. 'I need this gardening contract—more badly than you can possibly know—but I won't be bullied. And I won't be treated like this. It's not fair and I've had enough unfairness in my life to last a lifetime. More to the point, I won't have my family treated like that. My mum is already worried enough about me as it is. I'm not having you adding to it.'

She hit the camera icon and her mother came back into view. 'What happened, honey?'

'I think the connection up here is a bit…*dodgy*.' She glanced at Beau over the top of her laptop, letting him know that the only thing dodgy here was him. 'Hopefully, it's righted itself again now. And I expect I ought to get back to work, but I thought you might like to meet my employer, Beau.'

She sent him another pointed look and, with a scowl, he slouched over into view, but she noted he kept the scarred side of his face away from the camera.

'Hello, Mrs Jennings, it's nice to meet you.'

'Oh, it does put my mind at rest to meet you, Mr Diamond. And here you are looking so hale and hearty too!'

He stiffened and Chloe had to swallow a groan.

'You will keep an eye on Chloe for us, won't you, love? When she gets out in the garden she forgets all about the time and eating and whatnot.'

A slow—and she suspected somewhat reluctant—smile tugged at his lips, making her blink.

He crossed his heart. 'I promise to make sure she has three square meals a day. Besides, for the next few weeks she's also my housekeeper so she's going to have to learn to be a better timekeeper.'

'That all seems to have come a bit out of the blue.'

'It did, but my housekeeper's daughter is pregnant and suffering from morning sickness, and she wanted to be there for her over the holidays. I was grateful Chloe was able to step into the breach. I'm discovering that your daughter is a woman of…many talents.'

A cunning look came into her mother's eyes and she glanced at Chloe. 'Honey, why don't you get to work and leave me and Beau here to have a little chat?'

'Not a chance, Mum.' She pulled the computer back around to her and tried to push Beau away, but he proved immovable. 'I'm not letting you chew the poor man's ear off and give him a ton of instructions about what he ought to be doing and what I ought to be doing.'

'Oh, but—'

Beau turned the computer back towards him. 'Was there something specific you wanted to ask me, Mrs Jennings?'

'Yes, love. It's just…we're that worried about Chloe spending Christmas away this year.'

Chloe groaned and dropped her head to her hands.

'Christmas is a really big deal in our family. I mean, Chloe was even named for Christmas.'

'Ivy Belle,' he murmured.

'Exactly! Look, Beau, I know you must be a busy man, but can you find it in your heart to look out for our Chloe? Like I said, she'll work herself into the ground if you let her. And I understand her need to keep busy, but making herself sick won't help anyone.'

'No indeed.'

'Mum, I'm not going to get sick. I'm planning on having fun while I'm here. Adventure, remember?'

But her mother carried on as if she hadn't spoken. 'And if she's looking particularly glum… I don't know, maybe you could find a way to cheer her up a bit.'

Cheer her up? Beau!

She did her best to snort back a laugh. He had

myriad talents, but she doubted that was one of them.

'I'll do my best,' he managed.

'That's all I ask of you, pet. It eases my mind knowing she has someone there in Old Blighty who's looking out for her.'

Beau finally allowed Chloe to wrest back control of her laptop. 'You worry too much, Mum. Everything is going to be fine. I'll call you in a few days. I love you.'

'Love you too, sweetheart.'

She closed the lid of her laptop and moved towards the kettle. Finding Beau's proximity strangely disturbing. 'Tea?' Stephanie had told her he usually had a mid-morning tea and biscuit.

'Yes, please.' He was silent for a long moment. 'Why do you need the garden contract so badly?'

'None of your business.'

He huffed out a laugh. 'This isn't going to be a harmonious working relationship, is it?'

'Not shaping up that way,' she agreed, setting the tea to brew in the middle of the table and putting fingers of delicious-looking shortbread onto a blue china plate.

'Why is your mother so worried about you?'

She glanced up and raised an eyebrow.

He stared back and pursed his lips. 'Why do you need to keep so busy?' he tried instead.

She shook her head. 'Nope and nope.' And then gestured at the blue china plate. 'I've never made shortbread. So while Stephanie has left me her recipe, and I'm more than happy to give it a whirl, you might want to savour this while you can.'

'You don't have to do any baking. I'm just as happy with store-bought stuff.'

No way. Her eyes had nearly bugged out of her head when she'd read the figure she'd be receiving for filling in for Stephanie. She had every intention of earning it, which meant keeping both the biscuit and cake tins full while she was here.

'I liked your mum.'

She poured the tea. 'She liked you too.' The thought made her frown. Her mum was normally a good judge of character.

Actually, beside his ghastly suspicions, Beau was probably all right. But she hoped his temper didn't improve too much while she was here, because that meant she wouldn't have to put much of an effort into hers either. It was damn freeing not to have to feign politeness or fake friendliness or any kind of good cheer.

'That surprises you?'

What? Oh, her mum. 'Not really. She likes everyone.'

He rolled his eyes ceilingward. 'And now she's the queen of the backhanded compliment.'

One corner of his mouth hooked up, and she did what she could to ignore the discordant pitter-patter of her heart. Nobody could call Beau Diamond handsome, not any more. But that didn't stop his presence from feeling strangely dynamic. 'I've a whole repertoire of them. *And* I'm still waiting for your apology, by the way.'

'Look, Chloe, I have reasons for being so suspicious.'

She straightened. 'Of me?'

'Not of you.' He waved an impatient hand in the air. 'But I've been burned before.'

She could only imagine how much the press had hounded him after the accident. It was criminal the way some journalists behaved. But... 'That's not my fault.'

He halted with one of those delicious-looking shortbread fingers halfway to his mouth. She gave into temptation and reached for one too, bit into it and nearly groaned as the buttery goodness melted on her tongue.

'I mean, I'm sorry you've had people treat you like you were nothing more than a big news story, but it's not fair I pay the price for other people's sins.'

He set the biscuit down, but didn't say anything. For heaven's sake, she was just here to do a job, but how on earth was she supposed to convince him that was all she wanted?

Except that's not really true, is it, Chlo?

She bit her lip. 'You know, it'd be nice if we could be a bit friendlier to one another. I mean, if we're really going to be working on the garden together, side by side...' she tried to dismiss the images that flooded her mind '…then maybe we could even become friends.'

If they became friends and she told him why it was so important to her, surely he'd let her take a couple of photographs of the finished garden for her portfolio. Just in case she needed to apply for another contract like this one in the future.

His eyes narrowed as if sensing she had a hidden agenda. 'I don't need a friend, Ms Jennings. I just need you to do the job you were asked to do. Do I make myself clear?'

She needed the job so she nodded. 'Absolutely.'

He stalked out of the kitchen without drinking his tea, without eating his shortbread, and without a backward glance. 'So I suppose I can forget all about the apology you owe me,' she growled.

'I heard that!' he shouted down the hallway.

'You were supposed to!'

The exchange left her oddly energised, almost cheerful.

Beau scowled from the desk in his office when he saw Chloe marching across the courtyard towards the gardens a short time later, rugged up as if for an Arctic winter, her hands buried deep in the pockets of her coat, neck swathed in a scarf.

It's not fair I pay the price for other people's sins.

He swore. Her arrival was supposed to herald his resolution to get back to work. He might no longer be able to make the nature documentaries he so loved, but throwing himself into reclaiming the garden would help plug some of the ache in his soul. Her arrival, however, was also bringing home to him that Stephanie was right. He was in danger of becoming bitter and twisted.

To be perfectly honest, he wasn't all that interested in not being bitter and twisted, but Chloe was right—it wasn't fair that she pay the price for others' sins. Maybe she *was* looking for a way to exploit this situation, and he had every intention of keeping an eye on her, but cutting off that call with her mother and bellowing at her without giving her a chance to explain?

That made him a bully.

And he hated bullies.

The image of Chloe's mother rose in his mind, and he found himself fighting a smile. When was the last time someone had called him *love*? Mrs Jennings had a natural warmth he'd found himself drawn to. And it had felt oddly satisfying to pay Chloe back for forcing him to talk to her mother in the first place by refusing to gracefully fade into the background when she'd wanted him to.

Except it had backfired. He rubbed a hand over his face. What on earth had he actually promised?

To keep an eye on Chloe, to make sure she doesn't work too hard and to make sure she eats regular meals.

None of that would be too hard.

To cheer her up if she looks glum.

He glared at the ceiling. What on earth had possessed him to agree to *that*?

He was a fool, but Mrs Jennings's warmth and sincerity had taken him off guard. He'd found himself momentarily mesmerised by the maternal instincts that had driven her to ask for the favour in the first place, mesmerised by her evident love for her daughter.

She was so different from his mother and a part of him had yearned towards the older woman, had wanted to…? He didn't know how to finish that sentence. He had no idea what he'd wanted or what he'd been thinking. Maybe he was losing the plot?

He'd learned at the age of eight—when his parents had all but abandoned him—that the only person he could rely on was himself. It was a lesson he'd forgotten in recent years—to his detriment—when he'd started to trust in his colleagues' respect and the television network's high regard, had believed in his audience's admiration.

His lips twisted. He'd made the rookie mistake of believing his own press, but he'd learned his lesson. When life had gone pear-shaped none of them were to be found. Instead they'd left the gossip-mongers, scandal-hunters and voyeurs circling in their wake. Oh, yes, the message had been received loud and clear. *Rely on nobody* had been burned onto his brain.

None of that, however, meant he had the right to bully a woman like Chloe. And he was beginning to suspect that Chloe wasn't a woman on the make, but someone just searching for a bit of peace and quiet.

Like him.

He blew out a long breath, unanswered questions pecking away at him. Primary among them—why was Chloe *Ivy Belle* Jennings spending Christmas here in England with strangers when she could be enjoying it at home with her family?

Had she needed the garden contract so badly that when he'd suggested she arrive late November, she'd thought that akin to a royal decree?

Swearing, he lumbered to his feet and headed out into the gardens.

He tracked Chloe down to a corner of the walled garden and she turned to him, her face so alive and full of excitement it sucked the air from his lungs. With hair the colour of gingerbread, and eyes a shade darker, she looked like some autumn woodland nymph. An ache started up at the very centre of him.

She gestured. 'This is amazing.'

He glanced around and nodded. This garden was going to be his haven, his sanctuary. Here he'd be able to study the natural world, without interruption. He ground his back molars together. It *would* be enough.

'You are the luckiest man alive, Beau Diamond.'

Oh, really? It took a superhuman effort not to lift a hand to touch the scars on his face.

'Now you said something about wanting to attract wildlife to the garden,' she said, before he could apologise for his earlier behaviour. 'In my original design I suggested planting a mix of both wild and cultivated flowers. Are you still on board with that?'

'I want herbs in here as well.'

She pursed her lips. 'Swiss chard, thyme... sage.'

Perfect. He planned on spending long summer days out here, the flowers and grasses scenting the air as he tracked the different birds, butterflies and insects that the garden attracted.

'But you also want it to look pleasing to the eye. Did you want to keep the current configuration? I know it's desperately overgrown, but it has a pleasing symmetry.'

'I'd like to preserve as much as I can. But I want the addition of a water feature.'

'Any particular sort? Placed anywhere in particular?'

He shrugged.

'How about I sketch a few different designs and you can let me know what you like?'

Sounded good to him.

She turned on the spot, her mobile features

alive with an inner fire, and he wished her mother could see her face right now.

'I love that old tree down there.'

He glanced to where she pointed. 'It's an old hornbeam tree—good for shade.' It'd attract birds and insects too.

'This is going to be amazing once we're done. I can hardly wait to get started.'

He recalled Mrs Jennings's warning about Chloe working herself into the ground, and vowed not to let that happen. He adjusted his stance. 'Look, Chloe, you were right earlier. I do owe you an apology. I shouldn't have jumped to the conclusions I did. I shouldn't have ended your video call like that. It was…'

'An overreaction?'

But when he glanced at her, her eyes were dancing and he found his lips almost twitching into an answering smile. 'An overreaction,' he agreed. 'It's just…after you call out the police for the seventh time in three days to remove trespassers bearing cameras with telescopic lenses who've scaled the security fences, it does start to get old pretty quickly. Especially when you factor in the dozens of daily phone calls demanding an interview, and the fact that one's neighbours are also being inundated with opportunistic journalists and—'

She reached out and touched his arm. 'I'm sorry, Beau. I should've been more understanding.'

'No, you're just here to do a job—and I've already railroaded you into taking on additional duties. Understanding the external crap I have to put up with isn't part of your job description.' He was starting to suspect that Chloe had enough crap of her own to deal with.

'Are you still being hounded to that extent?'

'No, thank God.' And he didn't want anything reigniting media interest either. 'But I've learned the hard way to keep a keen eye out for anything suspicious.'

'I can see how you could've misconstrued what I said to my mother.' She started along the path towards the hornbeam tree. 'And, actually, I owe you an apology too because it's not my place to offer to show my family any of your lovely home. I was just...it's amazing and I wanted to share it with her. She's... I—'

He leaned in closer and she shrugged. 'I wanted her to see how much fun I'm having here.' She rolled her shoulders, not meeting his eyes. 'What an adventure it all is.'

She was a terrible liar. 'Chloe, if you want to spend Christmas at home with your family that's okay and—'

'No!'

She looked horrified by his suggestion. *Why?* Her mother was lovely.

So is your grandmother, but that doesn't mean

you want her descending on Dawncarden for the holidays.

His grandmother had provided some of the maternal nurturing he'd needed growing up, though her love had been brisk and no-nonsense rather than of the touchy-feely variety. He suspected Chloe's mum was touchy-feely to the core. He loved his grandmother, knew she loved him. But he didn't want her fussing and hounding him this Christmas. All he wanted was to be left in peace.

He glanced at Chloe and a surge of fellow feeling hit him.

Chloe straightened as if aware of his gaze. 'Beau, I want to assure you I won't invade your privacy like that and share photos of your house and grounds with my family. It's not my place and—'

'Look, I understand. No apologies necessary.'

She eyed him for a moment and he couldn't help wondering what she saw. Did she pity him for his scars? Did she find him repulsive?

He jerked away. He knew women no longer found him attractive. It didn't matter. None of it mattered.

'But it does bring me to something I want to raise.'

He turned back.

'When I was staying in the flat in the coach house, I had my own living space.' She twisted her hands together. 'You have a huge house and I just wondered… Would I be able to have a room, apart from my bedroom, that I can work in, and maybe stretch out in to watch the odd film on my computer?'

He should've thought of that. He couldn't give her Stephanie's suite, but… 'How big does it have to be?'

'No bigger than what was in the flat. But it needs to be an area where you wouldn't mind me video-calling with my family.'

He found himself staring at her hair, caught up in its shine and the richness of its colour. He snapped to, shook himself. 'I have just the space. Follow me.'

They'd reached the hornbeam, and he turned to lead them back the way they'd come, when a pungent odour pulled him up short.

'What on earth…?'

Chloe blinked. 'What on earth…what?'

Not paying her any heed, he ducked under the low branches of the hornbeam and searched the trunk and canopy, and then he caught a hint of movement by the wall. It was the western wall and…

'What are you—?'

He pressed a finger to his lips and, bending down slightly so she could follow the line of his finger, he pointed. 'Can you see?'

For a moment his attention wavered as he

caught her scent. She smelled of soap and lavender and for some reason it made his mouth go dry.

'What? I don't see anything— Wait!'

She clutched his arm and her excited whisper made his pulse quicken. She moved further beneath the canopy and then swung to him, her eyes huge and excited. 'It's a bat.'

CHAPTER THREE

'A PIPISTRELLE,' BEAU CORRECTED.

Chloe glanced at him. The volume of his voice hadn't risen above a whisper, but it vibrated with the same enthusiasm as when he'd filmed his documentaries. It hadn't mattered whether those documentaries had been filmed in the depths of a jungle or on some remote island off the coast of Ireland, in the Australian outback or the Serengeti Plains. Beau Diamond had a passion for the natural world in all its variations that his legion of fans had found irresistible.

'There's an entire colony here. I'm going to need to record numbers.'

She wanted to close her eyes and let the butterscotch warmth of that voice wash over her and—

She shook herself. Forced her eyes wide. 'These are rare?'

'Pipistrelle numbers in Britain have been falling. The places where they can safely roost have dwindled, as have their habitats.'

Which she guessed made it doubly important to preserve their current ones. Especially for a man like Beau.

'Chloe, this means things have changed.'

Her gut clenched. If he didn't want this colony disturbed, did that mean she was out of a job? The breath jammed in her throat. She *needed* this job. Not just for the money, even though that was the most pressing concern at the moment, but also for the prestige.

She and Mark had gone into business with his parents, and while the money from this contract meant she'd be able to keep her house, freeing his parents from any sense of obligation they had in relation to that particular debt, if the business should need a quick injection of funds in the future, she needed to pull her weight and find a solution—like attracting high-status design jobs that paid *really* well.

A weight slammed onto her shoulders. If only she'd known about the second mortgage Mark had taken out on the house. If only she'd read the letters his solicitor had sent earlier rather than falling into a bereaved mess and shoving them in a drawer and letting them stack up. If only Mark's parents hadn't shielded her for so long.

If only…

Her lips twisted. Life was full of 'if only', right? But she did know now. And it wasn't too late. She *could* turn things around. She didn't care what she had to do, but she *wasn't* losing the house—the last link to the husband she'd loved more than life itself. And there was no way she was letting the business carry her any longer. She was through with being a dead weight.

'Did you hear me?'

She swallowed the lump in her throat. 'Changes things how?' She glanced away from those piercing blue eyes, not wanting him to see the fear in hers. 'You no longer want to go ahead with the garden makeover?'

'What?'

He reached out as if to touch her arm, and her chest clenched. Instead, holding a finger to his lips, he led her away from the hornbeam tree that sheltered the piece of wall that had become home to a colony of pipistrelles. And while she was happy for them, she couldn't help but feel cursed.

'What the hell are you jabbering on about?' he demanded once they'd made their way into the middle of the garden.

Her head jerked up. This man had no idea how to do polite, did he? She gestured back the way they'd come. 'You don't want the pipistrelles disturbed, you want them to thrive, and I'm guessing that means you don't want any work taking place in the garden now.'

'Then you'd be guessing wrong.'

He stared at her as if she were a first-grade idiot and she found it oddly cheering. 'Oh?'

'We're going to turn this garden into a haven for pipistrelles, Chloe. Not to mention birds and butterflies.'

She tried to not sag too deeply in relief.

'But the design will now need to cater for what's

already living here. We won't be disturbing that pocket of the garden and the hornbeam tree stays.'

'Of course the hornbeam is staying,' she said, then winced at how bossy she sounded. Beau was the client. This was *his* garden. If he wanted the hornbeam gone, then that was what would happen. It wasn't her job to judge. 'I just mean…it looks as if it's been here a long time. There's a continuity to keeping it that—'

She broke off, reddening.

He raised an eyebrow. 'Go on.'

The words were uttered as an order rather than an invitation. She shook her head. 'You really need to work on your tone, Beau. No wonder Stephanie calls you *lord and master*. I'm not sure it *is* a joke.'

He blinked. 'You're calling me a bully again.'

It was her turn to blink. 'More like an autocratic grouch,' she hedged.

He stared at her with pursed lips and then shrugged. 'I suppose that's marginally better than being a bully.'

It absolutely was, but she kept her mouth firmly closed.

'Believe it or not, I've never been the most social of men.'

'I'd believe it.'

Her unguarded words, just as direct and rude as his, surprised a bark of laughter from him, and just for a moment she caught a glimpse of a younger, less guarded man.

'Well, believe it or not, even given my lack of sociability I once had a veneer of civility, but since moving back to Dawncarden that veneer has become somewhat rusty. I'm sorry if I sounded autocratic.'

Another apology. Wow.

'And I really would like to know what you were going to say about the hornbeam and continuity and what that signified to you.'

Her heart sped up though she had no idea why.

'Please?'

Pulling her coat around her more securely, she traced a path around the circular garden bed that lay at the heart of the garden, glancing back down towards the hornbeam. 'It just seems right to keep something that has been here so long. Just as your grandmother is the matriarch of your family, that hornbeam tree feels like the matriarch of this garden. It feels ethical to keep it.'

She glanced up to see if he was laughing and thinking her some weird hippy type. Instead he stared at the hornbeam with a light in his eyes that made her breath catch. 'I couldn't agree with you more. I knew you were the right person for this job.'

Her head came up and her shoulders went back. She was going to give him the best damn garden he'd ever seen.

'I want a pond.'

That sounded definite. 'Not a fountain?'

'Still water will attract insects, and bats feed on insects, among other things.'

Ah. She turned a slow circle. 'We could have a sunken pool there.' She pointed to the circular garden bed. 'And if you want we could have a small waterfall beside the wall over there, with a rill leading to the pond…and perhaps another rill leading to a smaller pool here.'

His face lit up. 'That sounds brilliant! Frogs would love it.'

Bats, birds, butterflies…and frogs, huh? She grinned as she saw what Beau wanted to achieve. He wanted to create a wildlife sanctuary here in this lovely hidden garden. A haven for whatever animals found their way. It'd be magical.

A quick glance informed her that his attention had once again returned to the far corner and the pipistrelles. She'd need to do some research on local wildlife. She'd pored over all the resources she'd accrued on English cottage gardens prior to applying for this contract, but that had been mostly plant based. She'd wanted to impress him, and she still did. She wanted to impress him so much he'd relax those crazy strict privacy policies he had and give her permission to take photographs of this finished garden for her portfolio. Behind her back, she crossed her fingers.

'You're itching to get back down there and count them, aren't you?'

'And to take photographs,' he confessed. 'I'm going to document everything I can about them. I want to see if, in the right conditions, that colony can grow. I want to know how many young they have. And in an ideal world I'd like to fit them with trackers. Though fitting trackers to pipistrelles is notoriously difficult, not to mention expensive.'

'You're going back to documentary making?' She only just stopped herself from jumping up and down on the spot and clapping. 'That's brilliant! It's—'

'*No!*'

The single word rang around the garden, and everything seemed to go suddenly quiet and still. She had to swallow before she could speak. 'But you just said…'

'I'm documenting this for my own edification, nobody else's.'

'But—'

'No buts.'

She slammed her hands to her hips. 'You could do so much *good*.'

His head rocked back.

'You could show people how to protect the country's pipistrelle populations, teach them how to coax pipistrelles into their gardens, and help them thrive and prosper.' How could he turn his back on that?

He gestured to his scars, his eyes chips of ice. 'Apparently this isn't the kind of face television networks want heading up their wildlife documentary series. My network made that very clear when they cancelled my series.'

Her heart froze before giving a giant kick. She leaned in, eyes wide. 'They dumped you because of your *scars*?'

He folded his arms, his face closed up.

But... 'Your fans don't care what you look like!' She gestured wildly. 'What they love is your enthusiasm and your unique take on the natural world, not—'

'Enough!'

She blinked at the savagery of that single word. The unfairness of what the network had done made her want to shred things with her bare hands and yell at someone. 'They're just one TV network, Beau. There are others—'

'No more.' He shoved a finger that shook beneath her nose and she discovered they were both breathing hard. He ought to smell of fire and brimstone, but he didn't. He smelled like a balsam fir, sharp and tangy, clean. She dragged the scent into her lungs.

A strange new energy flooded her and—

She took a hasty step back. *What on earth...?*
'Sorry. I got carried away. It's none of my busi-

ness.' What on earth was wrong with her? She needed to mind her Ps and Qs. She couldn't afford him cancelling her contract.

She walked across to one of the badly overgrown flower beds and picked a piece of wild rosemary that she lifted to her nose to try and chase the scent of him away. What a sorry pair the two of them were. She moistened her lips and half turned back towards him. 'Because you've been so rude to me, I've taken it for granted that I can be rude back, but clearly that's a juvenile attitude, not to mention unproductive.'

She trailed off, not sure what else to say. 'For various reasons that I won't go into, because... *boring*, I've had to put on a cheerful face back home, and I think the effort has burned me out. We both blamed jet lag for my outburst the other night, but...' Her eyes stung. 'The truth is I'm just too tired to be "nice" at the moment.' She clenched her hands. *You will not cry.* 'But I must try harder.'

'No.'

She turned towards him.

'You don't need to make any such effort for me.'

She had a feeling he meant it, but... 'I don't want to turn into that person, Beau—a bitter and twisted sad sack. I want to be able to like myself.'

A flash of scarlet caught her eye. She tracked it and then stilled. 'Look,' she breathed. 'A robin redbreast. Just like in the movie *The Secret Garden*. I've never seen one in real life.'

'What? *Never?*' He sounded utterly astonished, but then one broad and decidedly attractive shoulder lifted. 'Why would you? They're not native to Australia.'

'We don't get a white Christmas in Australia either, but I've always loved Christmas cards with robin redbreasts in the snow. They seem like such characters.'

'They are.'

She pulled her phone from her pocket to snap a picture, then remembered the privacy clause and shoved it back. Cool eyes surveyed her and she grimaced. 'Sorry, it's just a natural impulse to want to capture something like that.'

He pressed a thumb and forefinger to the bridge of his nose, looking suddenly old, and she had to fight an odd impulse to walk over and put her arms around him.

'Snap your picture, Chloe,' he said without lifting his head.

Before she could, the little bird flew away, which was probably just as well. She couldn't afford to accidentally contravene that privacy clause.

He let out a long breath. 'I promised to show you the room you could use while you're here.'

They walked back to the house in silence. Considering the words and apologies they'd just exchanged, the silence ought to have been fraught and uncomfortable, but it wasn't. There was something clean and honest about it. She'd discovered that they had a whole lot more in common than she'd realised.

Which wasn't the most comfortable of discoveries, but at least she now knew not to take his grumpiness personally. Hopefully he now knew the same about her.

He led her through that extraordinary baronial grand hall, and down a wide hallway. She knew his study was located at its far end, as Stephanie had showed it to her the previous day. He opened the second door on the right and gestured for her to precede him. 'Will this do?'

She walked in and then slammed to a halt, her jaw dropping. He'd just ushered her into the most magnificent library she'd ever seen outside a movie.

'This room has the big desk you'll probably need, and there's plenty of natural light.'

Light poured in at the three tall windows that overlooked the front oak-lined drive and sadly neglected rose garden that she itched to get her fingers on. The rest of the room was lined with floor-to-ceiling bookshelves. There was an enormous desk with a table lamp that would be the perfect spot for drafting her designs.

'And there are a couple of comfortable sofas for sprawling on when you want to watch a film.' Beau shoved his hands into his pockets. 'Will this do?'

'Do? It's perfect! It's the most wonderful room

I've ever seen.' She laughed and clapped her hands. 'We've just changed movies. I thought we were in *The Secret Garden*, but now we're in B—'

She broke off. Oh, God, what was she thinking? She wanted to bite her tongue clean out of her head.

Beau raised a for once civil eyebrow. 'And now we're in…?'

Beau did his best to keep a straight face. He was well versed in traditional children's stories and fairy tales or, at least, Disney's fairy-tale retellings. When he'd been growing up, he and his grandmother had shared regular movie nights. She'd insisted on Disney movies and romantic comedies, while he'd insisted on action movies and nature documentaries. It'd given them both an education.

So he knew exactly which movie Chloe had just cast herself in.

'I…uh…' She floundered, eyes wide, looking everywhere except at him.

'What fairy tale has a library…?' He tapped a finger against his lips. 'Could you possibly be referring to…' he forced his eyes wide, feigning outrage '…*Beauty and the Beast*?' Except his gut had started to churn. Was that how she saw him—as a beast? And even if she did, why did he care?

'I didn't mean it like that!' she burst out. 'I just meant that this is the most amazing library and I used to love to read, and I couldn't imagine a more wonderful room. *That's* all I meant. I certainly wasn't casting myself as Beauty and I wasn't implying that you're—'

He didn't say a word, but it took an effort to not laugh.

'Oh, look here!' She slammed hands on hips, eyes flashing fire. 'The only thing *beastly* about you is your temper!'

'Ditto,' he shot back, unable to hold in a laugh.

Her eyes narrowed. 'You have a warped sense of humour, you know that?'

'And you have a fairy-tale fetish.'

'Nothing wrong with a happy ever after, even if they do so rarely happen in real life.'

Her words had an ache stretching through his chest.

She glanced up at him. 'You're really not offended?'

'I'm not offended.'

She hesitated, and he waited, half fatalistically, for the next indiscreet, foot-in-mouth comment she was invariably about to make. He could stop her, he supposed, but her confession in the garden about having used up all of her reserves of niceness had slid beneath his guard.

He suspected what Chloe really needed at the moment was to snipe and vent. He might have a scarred face, but he also had broad shoulders. 'Out with it,' he ordered.

She wrinkled her nose, and it struck him that she had a cute nose, neat and pert with a sprinkling of freckles that somehow went with the gingerbread of her hair. She might not be considered a classic beauty, but she had the kind of face that made a man like him look twice.

Not that *that* meant anything.

'You don't see yourself as a beast, do you?' she blurted out.

'Of course not.'

Some of the hardness in her spine eased. 'Good. So your scars don't bother you?'

He tried to not take offence, but... 'You think I've shut myself away because I hate what I look like? You think I'm so vain I can't stand for the world to see me like this?'

She stared back. 'It's one interpretation that could be put on your retreat from the world.'

He went to deny it, but stopped and shot her a glare. 'You know that nothing we discuss here can be shared with anyone because of that privacy clause.'

'I know, I know, or you'll sue me for every penny...blah-blah-blah.' She flopped down on one of the sofas. 'We've established that already. Take it as read.'

'Fine.' He planted himself on the sofa opposite. 'Then perhaps there is an element of vanity to my hiding out here.'

She didn't look at him in sudden disgust, as

if he was weak or petty or any of those things, just nodded. 'It makes sense. You've always been handsome in the classic way of Cary Grant, Idris Elba and the Hemsworth brothers—flawless... gorgeous.'

She'd thought him gorgeous? Things inside him stood to attention. Then a bitter laugh rose through him. Thought—*past tense.*

'It was what you were known for, and—'

'I was known for my expertise!' He shot to his feet. 'And the fact I could make my subject accessible and interesting. Damn it, Chloe, I was a whole lot more than a pretty face and—'

'Ha! See?' She pointed a triumphant finger at him. 'I knew other things mattered more to you than your pretty face.'

He fell back down, scowling.

'But even so...' her eyes turned warm with sympathy '...there has to be an adjustment period.' Her gaze moved to his scars and she didn't bother trying to hide her scrutiny. It took an effort to remain in his seat. 'You're not perfect any more.'

'Oh, like that's a state secret!'

'So what? Welcome to the club. Ninety-nine per cent of us aren't perfect.'

He stilled.

'But you're not ugly, Beau, far from it. You're still a very attractive man.'

And then she frowned as if she found the realisation unwelcome.

He shook off the warmth her words created, refused to let them settle over him. 'Vanity isn't the main reason I've retreated to Dawncarden. I just… I hate the way the press treat me now—like I'm not a person, but a thing. I hate the lack of privacy. I really hate the lack of courtesy.' He was quiet for a moment. 'I hate the ugliness I've discovered in other people.'

Her eyes filled with sudden tears and he clenched his hands to fists. 'Don't you damn well cry, Chloe *Ivy Belle* Jennings.' He scowled at her. 'Why would you even do that?'

'It sucks that your network dumped you. I can't believe they did that.'

It had thrown him for a six. He'd needed somewhere private to lick his wounds. Call him naïve, but the fact the networks now saw him as incapable of doing his job because his face was no longer as pretty as it had once been had been a slap in the face he'd not been expecting. That was the real reason he'd retreated to Dawncarden.

All he'd ever wanted was to make nature documentaries. Bringing the natural world into the living rooms of the average person and sharing his wonder with them, making it clear how urgently the planet needed everyone to pull together if they weren't to lose valuable ecosystems and environments—it felt like what he was born to

do. Without that direction, he felt rudderless…
useless…*ugly.*

It was why he'd been so short with Chloe in the
garden when she'd suggested he return to documentary making. It was what he wanted with
every fierce fibre of his being, but that way was
closed to him now. And somehow he had to find
a way to accept that.

He rose. 'If you're happy with this room, then
I'll leave you to it. I need to get to work.'

'Let me guess—pipistrelle research.'

She'd got it in one.

'Thank you, Beau, this is perfect.' She rose too,
pressing her hands together. 'I am free to pop into
the village whenever I want, yes? I don't have
to order everything online. Or is that what you'd
prefer?'

'You're not under house arrest. You're free to
go wherever you want.'

'Right, well, there are a few things I need, so
I might pop down now. Then I'll get to work on
drafting my ideas for the water feature.'

'Okay, Dad, it was great to chat! Good luck at
golf tomorrow.'

Beau halted outside Chloe's room—which over
the last few days was what he'd started to call the
library. She'd sounded more cheerful than she had
since her arrival.

But when he glanced around the door—she

never closed it—she sat with her head resting on the closed lid of her laptop, making low groaning noises. He pursed his lips. Right. So not as cheerful as she'd made out, then.

He tapped on the door and she immediately straightened. 'Beau! Did you need something?'

He'd just wanted to let her know he was there. He just wanted... Rolling his shoulders, he gestured behind her. 'You've started decorating for Christmas.'

She glanced around. 'Oh, yes, well, it's the first of December and... I hope you don't mind?'

But as she turned back, her nose had curled and it made him frown. 'Why should I mind? You haven't got very far, though.' She'd only decorated the bookcases behind her with some holly and ivy, a fake Christmas tree with twinkling lights, and a gaudy plastic Santa. But as of yet the rest of the room was untouched.

She touched a switch and the sparkly lights of the tree immediately disappeared. Did she think he wouldn't like them? That they'd offend him somehow?

Well, where on earth would she get that idea?

The voice sounded suspiciously—and irritatingly—like Stephanie, but it had a point. Not a single Christmas decoration adorned Dawncarden—inside or out.

Chloe's mother's face rose in his mind. 'Would you like some help decorating the rest of the room?' They could make this space ooze with Christmas cheer. In their video calls, Chloe's mother would see this room all cheerful and Christmassy, and surely that would help ease her worry.

'No, thank you, I couldn't think of anything worse.'

She shuddered. She actually *shuddered*. What on earth…?

She shot to her feet. 'Cuppa?'

He'd just finished one, but he nodded anyway. He wanted to find out what was going on.

'So what's going on with the Christmas decorations, then?' he asked when they were seated around the kitchen table eating the last of Stephanie's shortbread. 'If you don't like them, why put them up?'

She blew out a breath. 'Can you keep a secret?'

'I'm a champion keeper of secrets.' He leaned towards her and that clean lavender scent hit him and a pulse came to life deep inside him. He bit back a curse, easing back again. 'But who on earth do you think I'm going to tell?'

'My mother if she ever catches sight of you in the background of one of my video calls home. Or if she ever calls here on the phone,' she added with an ominous lowering of her brows.

Questions started pecking away at him, insistent and impossible to ignore. 'You're right, you know? Sometimes you do have ferocious eye-brows.'

She blinked and lifted a hand to touch them.

'But as I'm never in the room whenever you video-conference with your family, and I *never* answer the home phone, I don't think you need to worry.'

She was quiet for a long moment, staring into her tea. 'I don't want my family worrying about me. I want them to think I'm having a ball this Christmas.'

'Right.' He drew the word out.

'I figured if they saw a few Christmas decorations in the background whenever we video-call it'll make them think I'm full of the spirit of the season, and that will put their minds at rest.'

He didn't know what he'd been expecting, but it sure as hell wasn't that. He set his mug down, his chest drawing tight. 'Why is your family so worried about you?'

He and Chloe hadn't exactly started off on the right foot, but somehow in the last week they'd settled into a comfortable routine. And when it wasn't comfortable, it was enlivening. It'd made him realise how bored he'd become. She had no reason to look on him as a friend, but...

He hadn't spoken so honestly to anyone in the last fourteen months as he had to her. It'd left him feeling lighter somehow...freer. If he could return the favour, he would.

She stared at him, those treacle-dark eyes stormy. She didn't want to discuss it, that much was clear, but she really shouldn't be bottling this stuff up—whatever it was. He chose his words carefully. 'You once told me I ought to consider therapy for my paranoia.'

She winced. 'I didn't really mean it.'

'Should I be finding you a therapist, Chloe? Does your family have a right to be concerned? You're living under my roof. That makes me responsible for you.'

'No, it doesn't!'

But when their gazes clashed, she was the first to look away.

'Fine! But can we walk while we're talking? I need the exercise and I was hoping to go and check out your orchard.'

'The orchard? Why?'

'A girl can dream, can't she?' She rose and wound a woollen scarf around her throat. 'You've a remarkable estate here. In my daily walks I've been exploring what I can and imagining what I'd do if it was mine and money was no object.'

It could be interesting to hear her thoughts. In the long term, he wanted the estate to become more self-sufficient.

They pulled on boots and coats and headed outside. 'You said you loved animals.'

The question made him blink. She gestured at him and then at their surroundings. 'Then where are they? Shouldn't you have a border collie at your heels and a fat contented tabby sitting by the fire inside? And a milking cow…and maybe a horse or two?'

'We've had all of those in the past, but when the last cat died, Stephanie wasn't ready to get a new one. And as for a dog… Well, when I was travelling so much, it didn't seem fair to leave one for other people to look after all the time.'

'But you're not travelling now?'

That was true.

They walked in silence until they reached the orchard. He glanced at her from the corner of his eye. 'So why is your family worried about you?'

She buried her hands deeper into the pockets of her coat. 'Two years ago my husband died and, well…'

His chest grew strangely tight at the sudden thickness in her voice. Chloe was a widow? 'Chloe, I had no idea…'

'There's no reason why you should.'

Except it felt wrong that he hadn't known. He rubbed a hand across his chest. It was clear she'd loved her husband. To have lost him… It didn't bear thinking about. 'I'm sorry, Chloe.'

She shrugged and sent him what he guessed was supposed to be a smile. 'Me too.'

'What happened?'

'A driver had a stroke at the wheel. The car

mounted the footpath and Mark was hit—killed instantly.'

He winced.

'At least he didn't suffer, that's what people said to me.' She huddled further into her scarf. 'As if that was somehow a blessing.'

She kicked a tuft of grass. 'Obviously I didn't want him to suffer. But why couldn't the car have mounted the path further down the road where nobody was walking? Or missed him by a hair's breadth? Or even have broken his legs? Being hurt would've been better than being dead.'

She was right, of course. No wonder she had so little sympathy with his self-pity and sense of injury.

His first impression had been the correct one. She'd barely noticed his scars. What she'd seen was a man who'd been involved in a terrible accident, but who had lived to tell the tale. From where she was standing, he was lucky. And for the first time in fourteen months, he had to agree.

CHAPTER FOUR

CHLOE GLANCED AT Beau and tried to not wince. He stared back as if afraid she might break or explode again like a firecracker.

She really had to stop doing that firecracker thing. The disaster that was her life wasn't this man's fault.

His forehead creased. 'So you miss your husband more at Christmas and that's why your family is worried?'

She pulled in a breath. 'Mark's death happened at this time of year.'

She saw rather than heard the breath that he expelled. Noted the way his body became larger as it pulled in another breath and held it. A body that held an undeniable fascination for her and—

She dragged her gaze away and focussed on the wooden fence they were approaching. Then blinked. 'A stile! I've read about them in Enid Blyton books and seen them in Jane Austen movies and things, but…' She shrugged, suddenly self-conscious. 'Sorry, it's just a bit of a novelty.'

'No stiles in Australia?'

She had no idea. 'I think we run more to cattle grids than stiles.'

She took the hand he offered as she negotiated it. Even through her mittens she could feel his heat and strength and it made her ridiculously aware of the breadth of his shoulders and the strength and power of those long legs and lean hips—

Stop it!

'Was the stile an attempt to change the subject?'

She reclaimed her hand. Why was he so interested in talking about Mark? And then she recalled his somewhat silly sense of responsibility towards her and had to smother a sigh. 'It wasn't, but I can't pretend this is my favourite topic of conversation. What do you want to know, Beau?'

That keen gaze raked her face. 'I liked your mum.'

'So you've already said.'

'You and your family are clearly close.'

'And…?'

'It makes me uneasy that you're lying to them.'

He didn't just look uneasy. He looked truly troubled.

The stile had led them into the orchard and she glanced around at the fruit trees, all winter bare and dormant—a lot like her—and huffed out a sigh. 'I just didn't want to ruin another Christmas for them, Beau. Christmas is a big thing for my family and…well, they deserve to celebrate the holiday without anything casting a blight on it.'

He started down an avenue. 'Obviously the Christmas Mark died would've been devastating for everyone.'

She kept easy pace beside him. 'My family

adored him. They were all shell-shocked.' While she'd been utterly devastated. 'And then last Christmas, obviously the worst of the shock had passed.' It had been a year, after all. 'But it was the first anniversary and... I don't know, it sent me into a spin.' She glanced up and grimaced. 'I basically spent three days crying.'

'Oh, Chloe.'

He reached out a hand as if to touch her, but she forced herself back into motion, forced her feet to cross to the nearest apple tree to study the suppleness of its branches, too tempted by the warmth and comfort he was offering. And she didn't want to be tempted by it. She didn't want to notice how virile and attractive Beau was or to begin fantasising about all the ways he could comfort her.

Not that he was offering anything more than a broad shoulder, of course. And she shouldn't be thinking about anything beyond that. But after two years of being on ice, those impulses were starting to thaw. In freezing cold Devon of all places!

She ducked beneath the branches of the apple tree, keeping it between her and Beau. 'The crying jag took me off guard. I didn't expect it to hit me so hard.' But the realisation that Mark was *never* coming back had hit her with such force she'd been helpless to fight it. 'It didn't matter that I told myself I was being self-indulgent and silly, I couldn't stop.'

She'd wrapped one hand around the tree's trunk and Beau wrapped his hand over hers, and while the trunk of the tree remained between them, he drew close and suddenly the tree seemed no barrier against him at all. 'You were entitled to your grief, Chloe. Those sorts of things should never be bottled up.'

She stared at that perfect mouth, bracketed on either side with creases that lent the face strength, and her heart gave a giant kick that knocked the breath from her body.

She reefed her hand from beneath his and took a step back, rubbing her chest. 'Mark's death and then my grief have ruined the last two Christmases.'

'And you were afraid you'd ruin this one as well?'

Actually she'd been doing rather well. Had started to find her feet, had started to look forward to things again—playing with her nephews and nieces, family barbeques, nights out with friends. She'd even started to look forward to Christmas. She'd thought that this year she could turn a corner and set her face firmly towards the future as her mother had been urging her to do.

But then *wham*! She'd received the registered letter from the bank telling her about the second mortgage Mark had taken out on their home and that she was in imminent danger of losing everything the two of them had worked so hard for.

And all of her newly hatched optimism had been pulverised to dust.

Mark's family had confessed that he'd taken out the second mortgage to help the business stay afloat. They'd been trying to keep up with the additional payments, but had fallen behind. They'd been doing their best to shield her from it all this time because of her grief. They hadn't wanted her spiralling further into depression.

Dear God, they'd been carrying her financially and she'd been doing nothing to help!

It would've been impossible for her to pretend that everything was okay this Christmas. Her family would know something was wrong if she were there in person. And she wasn't wrecking another Christmas or casting a shadow on their celebrations. Just...*no.*

'I didn't want to risk it,' she finally said. 'This year I want them free from worry. They deserve to have fun. I think they need it. And my argument that I needed a change of scene made sense to them, even if they weren't enthusiastic about it. And I feel I'll be doing my part in making sure they have a good Christmas if I can show them what a great time I'm having here.'

'Even if it's a lie?'

She gave a hard nod. 'Yep.'

They'd started walking down another avenue. She studied the trees growing either side. 'You have apple, plum...cherry.'

'And pear and quince.'

She turned on the spot. 'It's badly neglected, but most of it can be saved, and you really ought to make that a priority, Beau. I suspect you have some heirloom trees here...and you have a duty of care.' Once trees like that were lost, they were lost for good.

His face had turned grim and she reminded herself she was here as his garden designer, not to lecture him about his orchard. She made herself smile. 'Of course, that all takes money. And money isn't always readily available.' It must cost a fortune to maintain Dawncarden Court.

'The money's available. The estate has one of the largest dairies in Devon. It's just...'

'You don't want workmen invading your privacy.'

He stared up at the sky and then at her. 'You wouldn't want the job of head gardener by any chance, would you?'

To bring this orchard back to life, not to mention the rose gardens, and to see the walled garden flourish would be...

She swallowed and shook her head. She needed to see this contract through, collect the big dollars it would bring in and then return to Sydney to help the business get back on a secure footing. She needed to pay that second mortgage off, and the sooner the better.

If necessary she'd apply for more contracts like

this one. But if she was to win them, she was going to need a portfolio that would impress potential clients. She glanced at Beau and bit her lip. A portfolio with before and after photographs of the projects she'd worked on.

He'd stopped and was staring at something in the middle distance. 'You know you could be onto something? My grandmother swears she's spending this Christmas with friends in Florence, but…' He tapped a finger against that perfect mouth. 'I'm not yet convinced that she won't descend on Dawncarden instead.'

'Would it be bad if she was to show up?'

'Don't get me wrong, I love my grandmother.'

'But?'

He raised an eyebrow, those blue eyes piercing. 'Would it be a bad thing if your family were to show up here this Christmas?'

She forced her legs back into motion. 'Point taken.'

'But if I decked out the hall the way it used to be when I was a boy and sent her a few photographs…'

Those long legs kept easy pace beside her. She ordered herself not to notice his legs.

'Maybe it'd stop her worrying about me so much.'

Ugh, time to come clean. 'I, uh, spoke to your grandmother earlier this morning.'

He nodded. 'She mentioned something about calling you in her last email.'

She let out a breath. Good, that wasn't supposed to be a secret, then.

'But back to decorating the hall, it also has the advantage of you being able to tell your family that you did the decorating and to share the pictures.'

A jolt went through her. 'You'd let me do that?' Maybe it wouldn't be so hard to convince him to let her photograph his garden for her portfolio after all.

'Why not? I think we can help each other out. It's all in a good cause.'

'We just want our families to be happy and have a nice Christmas.'

'Exactly. That's worth going to the trouble of putting up a few decorations, right?'

'Absolutely!' Oh, her mother would be so relieved. For a moment she was tempted to hug him.

Instead she took a step back and tackled the topic of his grandmother. 'Your grandmother made me promise to report in to her.'

His lips twisted. 'She informed me of that too.'

Her shoulders sagged. 'You think I'm a traitor.'

That made him laugh. 'I think nothing of the sort. I *know* my grandmother, Chloe.'

'She said she'd made a deal with you. That she'd let you remain on the estate unmolested by her interference as long as you went into the village twice a month.'

'She'd have let me stay, even if I hadn't made the promise, but I knew she was worried about me and it seemed little enough to ask.'

He might've come across as all grumpy and self-absorbed initially, but she was starting to see that, beneath his gruff exterior, Beau had a kind heart. 'But... What about the press?'

He glanced at her. 'I grew up here. And while I did go away to boarding school, I spent all of my summers here.'

She halted, slapped a mittened hand to her brow. 'The villagers protect you from the press.' She glared. 'And send unsuspecting garden designers on wild goose chases?'

He grimaced. 'Sorry about that. Steph and I got our wires crossed. But, yes, I'm warned if there's anyone suspicious about. And twice a month I spend a quiet hour or two over a pint of bitter in the snug at The Nag's Head—the smaller and less fashionable of the two pubs in the village. And as the hotelier is an old friend...'

'He makes sure no one disturbs you.'

'Exactly.' He suddenly halted. 'Except there hasn't been anyone from the press here in the last three or four months.'

'Clearly you're old news.'

He frowned and it occurred to her then that he

didn't find that news as welcome as he'd thought he would.

He shook himself and they started walking again. 'They do a few Christmassy things in the village too. My grandmother has spies in Ballingsmallard who report back to her whenever they see me, so it might be an idea to attend the village tree lighting. There are also Christmas markets.'

Something in her chest lifted. 'Christmas markets?'

'You should go, take a few selfies. Your family would love to see you in an archetypal English Christmas setting.'

She wrinkled her nose. Yeah, like walking around the markets on her own with all of that ghastly Christmas cheer in the air would be fun. *Not.* His grandmother was right, though. Beau needed to get back out into the world again. 'I'm only going if you go too. I'm not mooching around like a Nigel-No-Friends on my own.'

His nose curled, and he rolled his shoulders. 'We can think about it.'

'Deal.'

'And speaking of deals.' Those blue eyes, oddly warm, met hers. 'You will help me decorate the hall, won't you?'

'Absolutely.' She'd do anything to ensure her family didn't worry about her this Christmas. Even if that did mean going to Christmas markets on her own.

'C'mon. You've had ample time to check out the orchard and you're clearly cold. Let's get up into the attic and bring the decorations down. I'll need you to order a tree for delivery too.'

She gave a mock salute, but his sudden sense of purpose lifted something inside her. Beau Diamond might think he wanted to shut himself away in his castle—okay, maybe Dawncarden wasn't exactly a castle, but it was a grand old manor house, which was the next best thing—but the first stirrings of interest in the outside world were making themselves felt and she had no intention of doing anything that would undermine them. In fact, she had every intention of doing what she could to encourage them.

The world needed Beau Diamond.

And Beau Diamond needed the world. She was sure of it.

Beau stood in the corridor and listened to proceedings in the baronial hall and had to smother a grin as Chloe directed the deliverymen to set the Christmas tree into the stand waiting for it beside the stairs. When they'd realised they weren't going to catch a glimpse of the famous recluse, they'd clearly hoped to drop the tree off and make a quick getaway, but she was having none of it.

While her accent was altogether different from Stephanie's, she had obviously decided to channel the older woman's no-nonsense approach with a dash of her own practical flattery. 'Given how much you're charging Mr Diamond for the tree, the least you can do is place it in the stand there. Three burly chaps like you? It'll take you no time at all. And there's fruit mince pies waiting for once you're done.'

From the huffing and puffing that ensued, he guessed she'd convinced them to do as she asked.

'*What* do you think you're doing?'

Her tone of voice had him instantly stiffening, and ready to leap to her aid.

'I...uh...just thought...'

'Put that phone away right now! You do not have permission to take pictures of either the inside or outside of Dawncarden Court. Do I make myself clear? In fact, I'm going to speak to your boss about this and—'

'I'm the boss, miss,' another voice cut in, 'and I can't apologise enough.'

'Have any of you taken pictures while my back was turned?'

She sounded fierce. He'd bet she was using those eyebrows to full effect. The thought made him grin.

'Right, lads, show the lady your phones so she can see there aren't any photos of Dawncarden Court on them. And if I see any of you with your phones out again you'll receive an official warning.'

'Thank you,' Chloe said a moment later, 'and thank you. And now yours.'

'Mine?' the older man spluttered.

But he must've shown her because a few moments later she murmured another, 'Thank you,' and they left.

He emerged from the corridor and she gestured at the tree. 'It's magnificent! I thought ours at home was big, but this one has to be five times as big.' She checked the branches and the trunk. 'It's nice and healthy too.'

'You did a great job, just then, Chloe.'

She glanced at him over her shoulder and there was something about that gingerbread hair backlit by the green of the tree that had him thinking of woodland groves.

'Oh, so you heard all that?'

She shrugged as if it was no big deal, but it touched him that she'd taken such pains with his privacy.

'I'm the youngest of four. When you have three older siblings, you learn to hold you own.'

He reached out and ran his fingers across the needles of a nearby branch, the scent of lavender and fruit mince pies rising up around him, merging with the scent of pine, and his senses jolted to sudden wakeful life.

'If the truth be known, I just channelled Stephanie.' One shoulder lifted. 'It seemed to work.'

She could say that again. He caught her glancing at him with a question in her eye that was quickly shut off. 'What?'

She shook her head a little too quickly.

'Ask your question, Chloe.' He'd surrendered to the fact that their relationship was going to be far from comfortable, but he found himself trusting her, and that was far more important. Chloe wasn't the kind of person who'd sell him out. She had more important things to worry about.

'If someone did snap a picture of an undecorated tree in Dawncarden Court's baronial hall, would it be worth much?'

'I suspect it wouldn't cause much of a sensation. But now that media interest has waned, I don't want anything reinvigorating it.' Especially not if he was planning on dragging Chloe out to the village in the interest of reviving her Christmas spirit.

Was he really going to do that?

She nodded towards the tree. 'You know, if you snapped a before and after pic of that and put it on your Instagram account, nobody would be able to make any money from it whatsoever.'

He snapped upright. '*Not* going to happen.'

'Fair enough. Just as long as you know it's in your power to beat the tabloids at their own game and normalise your life.'

There was nothing *normal* about his life.

'And give your fans a few scraps.'

He didn't have fans any more.

'So…' She dusted off her hands. 'The sooner we decorate this monster, the sooner it's done.'

He fought the urge then to brace his hands on his knees. The way she said it, as if it were a chore, was a tragedy. This woman had once loved Christmas. Did she really find it so onerous now?

He forced steel to his spine. 'Wait until you see some of these old decorations. They're pretty amazing—even to someone like me who doesn't care one way or the other about Christmas.'

They'd brought all of the boxes down the previous afternoon and had stacked them beside the huge fireplace.

He glanced at her again. Despite her current jaded mood, surely she couldn't help but be impressed by Dawncarden's baronial hall decked out for Christmas, especially with a fire crackling in that venerable hearth.

'Right.' Chloe grabbed the closest box and hauled it over to the tree. 'How are we going to do this? Just chuck whatever decoration comes to hand wherever? Or do you have a system? We used to—*oh!*'

She'd unwrapped the first of the decorations—a coloured glass reindeer—and stared at it in awe. He stifled a smile. 'Pretty, right?'

'This isn't just pretty, Beau. This is *stunning*. A collector's item or...' She suddenly thrust it at him. 'It's probably an antique and worth a fortune! I really shouldn't be handling these. I'd die if I broke one and—'

'Absolutely! It's a capital offence. If you break

anything you'll be sent straight to the tower and beheaded in the morning.'

A reluctant smile tugged at her lips and it lightened the heaviness inside him. He wanted her to relax…to have fun.

'Breakages happen. It's called natural attrition.'

These were just things. Things could be replaced. People couldn't. The image of the grief raw on her face when she'd spoken about Mark rose once more in his mind and his gut clenched. She'd clearly loved her husband. No wonder her mother was still so worried about her.

He could do nothing about the loss of her husband, but bit by bit he might be able to bring back some of her Christmas mojo. It seemed the least he could do after all of his ugly suspicions and bad temper.

And getting the great hall decorated was the first item on that agenda. Surely seeing something so grand and festive every day couldn't help but have an impact on her Christmas spirit. 'Don't you think it'd be a shame if these were locked away and never saw the light of day, that nobody had the chance to enjoy them just because someone was afraid of breaking them?'

'I suppose so, but I don't want to be *that* person—the clumsy one that goes down in family lore. "Oh, and the matching pair to this irreplaceable antique glass reindeer was smashed by the lowly gardener of the tenth Baron of Dawncarden, though what on earth he was doing allowing her in the house in the first place is a mystery.'"

He couldn't help laughing at her nonsense. 'Would it help if I broke one first?' He made as if to toss a beautiful glass bell towards the fireplace. 'Would that ease your mind?'

'Don't you even think about it!'

Leaping forward, she rescued the bell from his fingers, and for a moment it felt as if he was grasping an armful of warm woman and endless possibilities. But then she stepped away and he thudded back to earth and he told himself to stop being an idiot.

'You channelled Steph perfectly when the deliverymen were here. Channel her again now. I can assure you these don't hold any fear for her whatsoever.'

Her face lightened. 'I so want to be Stephanie when I grow up.'

'Why?'

'She's so...together.'

He laughed and shook his head. 'We'll start with the lights. I'll go up the ladder, and you can pass them up. Then we can get started on the ornaments. I'll do the higher branches and you can do the lower branches. How's that for a plan?'

'Works for me.'

Reaching into his pocket for his phone, he streamed Christmas music through the sound system. She glanced up when it started crooning through the speakers, and rolled her eyes, but didn't say anything.

But when she eventually started humming along, stepping back to survey the tree with her designer's eye, a smile opened up inside him. He didn't completely understand his desire to help her recover her Christmas spirit. It was more than the promise he'd made to her mother, and it was more than an apology or attempt to make up for his earlier bad-tempered suspicions.

He'd been feeling powerless, but Steph's words had left a mark. He wanted to prove that he could still do some good, could make a difference in a positive way. He didn't want to turn into some bitter and twisted shadow of his former self. He just wanted the world to leave him alone to follow his own course.

Besides, Chloe had reminded him that some people really wouldn't care about his scars. He'd become so suspicious of everyone he'd forgotten that. He'd only been able to focus on those who now thought him a freak, or, if not a freak, then damaged goods. If he could surround himself with people who didn't care about his scars…and not even surround, but just have a couple of them in his life, then he could relax his guard and just get on with his research and find a bit of purpose again.

Her audible gasp brought him back to earth.

'Oh, Beau!' She turned with the tree-topper—

an angel—held reverently in her hands. 'I've never seen anything more beautiful.'

It occurred to him that angels were always blonde and serene. But what was wrong with a gingerbread-haired angel with a sprinkle of freckles across her nose and a glint of mischief in her treacle-dark eyes? Actually, the more he thought about it, the more he wanted that angel at the top of his tree rather than the one Chloe held in her hands.

He stared at it and then at her. 'Why don't I video you putting the angel in place? You can send it to your family.'

Her entire face lit up. 'Really? You wouldn't mind?'

He liked Mrs Jennings, and he was on board with Chloe's plans to help her family have a Christmas free from worry. 'Pass me your phone.'

She pulled it from her pocket and then paused, consternation flashing across her face. 'I have a few pictures of your garden on my phone. They're just to help me as I draw up my new designs. Not for any other purpose. I'll delete all of them before I leave, and you can watch me do that if you want. I don't want you thinking—'

'Relax, Chloe, I trust you.'

She blinked and then moved closer to peer into his face. 'You do?'

'Yes.'

She didn't say anything so he rolled his shoulders. 'I don't believe you're the kind of person who would sell me out to the tabloids.' Instead she was the kind of woman who was trying to cope with the death of a husband she still desperately missed. She didn't care about his paltry cares and concerns, beyond giving him the garden of his dreams. 'I thought I'd already made myself clear.'

'Well, I know it's what you said, but...'

She hadn't believed him. He suddenly hated how he must appear to her—and this time he wasn't referring to what he looked like physically. Plucking her phone from unresisting fingers, he gestured towards the tree and the ladder. 'I'll hold it steady while you go up.'

Once she was in place, and steady, he videoed her placing the angel on top of the tree. She then climbed down the ladder to gesture at the finished tree with an almighty, 'Ta-da!' Clapping her hands, she grinned madly at the camera. 'Isn't it the best?'

Her excitement couldn't be wholly feigned, could it? His heart thumped as her smile and her lips filled his vision. His blood began to beat out a primitive rhythm, making things inside him draw tight.

She took her phone and watched the piece of video. 'Oh, Beau, this is brilliant! I can't thank you enough. My family—'

She glanced up and her words petered out as their gazes caught and clung. Her eyes widened at whatever she saw in his face, she swallowed… and then her gaze lowered to his mouth and her eyes darkened and her lips parted as if she found it suddenly difficult to breathe.

A fierce primitive joy surged through him, taking him completely off guard. He'd never expected a woman to look at him again with such naked hunger—hadn't dared hope such a thing would be possible. But in that moment he understood that Chloe wanted him every bit as much as he did her. Something in her blood spoke to his.

Their uncomfortable and challenging working relationship hadn't been due to their bad tempers after all, but the physical attraction developing between them. When she was near, his body came alive in a way it hadn't in a long time and he ached to find the kind of release with her that his every instinct told him would be sensational. He wanted to give her that same release.

He reached out to touch her face—gently. She reminded him of some shy woodland creature that would start at any sudden movement. He didn't want to frighten her.

He wanted to give her time to catch up with him, and then he wanted to taste every delicious millimetre of her lips—slowly, thoroughly and without rushing. He wanted to give her the kind of mindless pleasure that would chase all the sadness and worry from her mind for a few short hours.

What would she taste like—honey and ginger? Would she kiss him back gently or fiercely? Would she wrap her arms around his neck and press that sweet body against his?

The sweetest song sang through his veins when she moved a fraction closer and he felt as if he'd stretched out giant wings—not like an angel, but an eagle—and soared on deliriously exhilarating air currents.

CHAPTER FIVE

HAD HER PULSE ever fluttered so wildly? Had her heart ever pounded so hard? As Chloe stared at Beau's bewitching mouth, things inside her thrashed and crashed like a wild horse trying to break free of a lasso. He wanted to kiss her. And she was going to kiss him back. Every instinct she had told her that the experience would be wild and fabulous and freeing.

They stood there, poised between heartbeats, relishing the—

Mark.

His name whispered through her mind. She could almost see the printed letters form in front of her face, which then dissolved to reform into capital letters. MARK! And then they became arrows spearing into her with deadly accuracy.

She flinched.

'No!'

The word sounded unnaturally loud in the silence of the room.

'No!' she shouted again, which was completely unnecessary because it was clear from how quickly Beau had dropped his hand and stepped back that he'd heard her the first time.

She stabbed a finger at him. 'This can't happen. It can *never* happen.'

Wheeling away, she started for the stairs, achingly and boilingly furious. Not at Beau, but at herself. How could she have even thought about kissing another man? How could anyone ever replace Mark in her heart?

They couldn't!

Sex and love aren't necessarily synonymous.

She batted the traitorous thought away as she stumbled up the stairs. She'd loved Mark with her whole heart and if she couldn't have sex with him then she didn't want to have sex with anyone.

Liar.

'Chloe, wait!'

Something in the urgency of Beau's voice pulled her to a halt.

'Please don't run away as if you're scared of me. Please let me apologise.'

She hauled in a breath. 'I'm not scared of you, Beau. I just need to get away before I hurl ugly awful things at you, things that you don't deserve, things that have more to do with me than you and—' She broke off with a frown. 'Not *thing* things, but words…accusations—'

'I don't mind if you do.'

He had no idea. If he did, he wouldn't be so blasé.

'And maybe I do deserve them.'

He leapt lightly up the stairs, stopping a couple of steps below her, allowing her to maintain the height advantage—not touching her, leaving her free to flee if she wanted to. His pallor and the way the lines around his mouth had deepened made her stomach churn.

'Please allow me to apologise. There's been enough media attention and the whole #metoo movement to educate men in positions of power to not put employees in compromising positions.'

Hold on. *What?*

'I apologise unreservedly for putting you in that position and for making you feel uncomfortable. I hate myself for it. And let me assure you that your contract and your position here are in no danger whatsoever of—'

She leaned forward. 'What on earth are you blathering on about?'

'Abusing my position here as your employer and making you feel pressured and—'

She waved both hands in front of her face. 'Look, I don't exactly see you as my boss, okay? I'm my own boss. You're my client. You've simply contracted me to do a job. We signed a contract. If you break it, I can sue you.'

He blinked.

'And if I break it, you can sue me. I don't feel there's a power play happening here. I mean, I know I'm acting as your housekeeper, but that's more as a favour.' She shrugged. 'I know you're paying the housekeeper's wage, but…' Her frown deepened. 'You know, the power in that arrangement feels as if it rests with me.'

He raised an eyebrow.

'*You* want me to be housekeeper more than *I* want to be housekeeper. I could probably behave really badly and take advantage of you, but as long as I don't sell you out to the papers I suspect I'd get away with it.'

His lips twisted as if acknowledging the hit.

'So that—' She waved her hand to the spot beside the tree where they'd—

She shied away from finishing the sentence, from putting into words what they'd almost done. 'It had nothing to do with power plays, so stop already with the self-flagellation.'

His gaze raked her face, and the lines around his mouth eased. 'So I didn't scare you?'

'No.' She'd scared herself. *That* was the problem.

'And you didn't feel pressured by me or in fear that your job and contract were in any danger?'

'No.' The thought hadn't crossed her mind.

Because you were too busy lusting after him.

How could she let herself do that? How could she let herself get so caught up in the moment? It was too soon—

Chlo, it's been two years.

She ignored that too.

Reaching up, he pushed a strand of hair that had worked free from her braid back behind her ear. 'Then, Chloe, what was that about? The expression on your face froze my bone marrow.'

Good! Hopefully it'd mean he'd never try to kiss her again. 'I don't want to talk about it. And you can't make me!'

Dear God, did she have to sound so juvenile and immature?

He eased down a step. 'No, of course not.'

The expression on his face made her feel like a heel.

'I have things to do,' she blurted out and then she turned around and fled.

It was no use! She couldn't sleep.

The Daffodil room was gorgeous—all warm yellow and wood panelling, with a four-poster bed boasting luscious brocade drapes. It was the kind of bed fit for a princess. But she couldn't appreciate it tonight. Tonight her mind was filled with Beau.

When she closed her eyes she saw his face, imagined his hands on her body doing things that made her shift restlessly against the sheets. She wondered what it would be like to run her hands down the intriguing lines of that masculine body—testing the firmness and strength of his flesh—and her fingers flexed.

That moment by the tree... They'd almost kissed. And if they had—

Her eyes flew open and a deep ache gripped her. If she was prepared to throw caution to the wind—

She sat up, dragging her hands through her

hair. *Stop it.* Think of Mark. Wanting another man should be a betrayal of the love she'd felt for her husband. Burying her face in her hands, she shook her head. But that wasn't how she felt. And she didn't know what it meant.

Letting out a long breath, she straightened and tried to channel calm. She knew that *technically* lusting after another man, or even sleeping with someone, wasn't betraying Mark. During the course of the last two years she'd been forced to acknowledge that she'd have to go on without him.

And clearly her body was still alive. She was young. This was a normal hormonal reaction. She gritted her teeth. Eventually all of this heated longing, the prickling and throbbing, would go away again. She just needed to wait it out.

Fine. If she couldn't trust her body to behave, then she needed to focus her mind. She might've lost Mark but that didn't mean she was prepared to lose the life they'd worked so hard to build—the house, the business. Thoughts of losing what little she did have left of her husband slowly chased the heat from her body, the fears and worries circling her mind like sharks instead—threatening, ominous…devastating.

Dear God, they weren't going to help her sleep either.

'Enough already.' She threw the covers back with a growl and planted her feet firmly on the floor. She'd make a cup of cocoa, sip it calmly, and then come back and do some relaxation exercises. It was her own fault for having retreated to her bedroom so early. That had been foolish.

But after a far from comfortable dinner with Beau where they'd attempted stilted conversation over the shepherd's pie, it'd been a relief to finally clean the kitchen and retreat to her own little haven. It had seemed like a smart plan. Except thoughts of him had continued to plague her.

Her bedroom was to the right of the stairs. Beau's was to the left. Six doors separated his bedroom from hers. Unless she slammed her door and shouted at the top of her voice, slipping downstairs at midnight shouldn't disturb him.

Nevertheless, she was careful to open her door quietly and start the descent down the stairs on silent tiptoes. It wasn't until she reached the landing at the turn of the stairs that she realised the man who'd occupied her thoughts for most of the evening sat on the third step from the bottom. He stared at the ridiculously beautiful Christmas tree, lights twinkling and the multitude of decorations sparkling, with hunched shoulders and a bowed head.

She could tiptoe back the way she'd come. He'd be none the wiser...

But something about those hunched shoulders caught at her. She'd been mired in a hell of grief for so long it occurred to her that maybe she'd grown callous towards the griefs and hardships of others. The thought made her frown. She didn't want to become that kind of person.

She forced herself down the stairs to sit beside him, though not too near. 'Can't sleep?'

He glanced around and shook his head.

She bit her lip. 'Are you still beating yourself up about earlier?'

'No.' He straightened. 'Should I be?'

'Absolutely not!'

He glanced back at the tree. 'I'll admit I found it…confronting.'

She winced. 'My temper has a mind of its own at the moment. That's on me, though, not you.'

His smile didn't reach his eyes. 'It wasn't your temper that was confronting, Chloe. Besides, you didn't really lose it, you know?'

Hadn't she? It had felt as if she had. Inside she'd felt as if she'd been hurling things at the wall, totally out of control.

'What I found confronting…'

Perfect lips twisted, and she dragged her gaze away, ignored the pulse that started up deep inside. Broad shoulders lifted. *Nope, not noticing them either.*

'It felt as if I'd come alive again, and that felt wonderful. And then, clearly, it didn't. When you backed off so quickly I worried I'd come on too strong, had misconstrued every signal. And I'm still worried I did—'

She touched his arm to halt his words. 'You

didn't misconstrue anything, Beau.' She dragged her hand back into her lap, fingertips tingling. 'It's just… I'm not ready for anything like that yet.'

He stared at her for a moment and she had the oddest feeling he wanted to challenge her. She let out a breath when he let it pass. 'So that's why you're feeling gloomy? Because you thought you'd misread me?'

'I never thought a woman would find me attractive again. And when you retreated, I thought I'd been indulging in a serious case of wishful thinking.'

He was talking now about his scars, thinking most women wouldn't see past them. It took an effort not to yell at him. 'Most people aren't as shallow as you seem to think.'

He stared at his hands. 'I didn't realise I'd be prepared to take the plunge and risk rejection.'

He thought she'd rejected him?

You did reject him.

But not because he was scarred! 'Beau, I don't want you thinking—'

'I don't.'

'You don't know what I was going to say.'

'I know my scars don't bother you.'

Really? One glance into those piercing blue eyes and she found herself nodding. *Good.* 'Then what has you so gloomy?'

He shifted and she realised she didn't want him getting up and walking away. Who had he had to confide in recently? He was so isolated here at Dawncarden, and while she knew it had nothing to do with her, it made all the sore places inside her ache. She wanted to help. If she could.

'I'd like to know,' she added quietly.

He let out a low breath, nodded at the Christmas tree and then lifted a photograph album. 'I was looking through this. It's from the Christmas when I was seven. I wanted to see how the hall was decorated back then. I had some crazy notion that I could recreate it.'

She took the album and turned the pages. *'Oh!* It looks magical.'

'But as I was flicking through, I suddenly realised how much I've been worrying my grandmother.' He pointed. 'That's her there.'

She was a tall, angular-looking woman with piercing eyes just like her grandson's. Everything about her screamed rigid respectability, but her smile was kind. 'I like what she looks like.'

'That's my mother and father.'

He'd received his dark thick hair from his mother and his perfect mouth from his father.

'When my father's business failed he turned to drugs.'

She stared at him, her mouth falling open.

'My mother had a kind of nervous breakdown and has since retreated to some ashram in India where she eschews her old life and goes by a different name.'

'Is your father still alive?'

'He overdosed, but the paramedics eventually managed to revive him. His brain was starved of oxygen for too long, though, and now he's more child than man. He's in a clinic receiving the best of care, but doesn't really recognise anyone any more.'

'Oh, Beau, I'm so sorry! How old were you when this all happened?'

'Eight.' He nodded at the album. 'The year following that Christmas.'

Here she was feeling ridiculously sorry for herself—and angry at him for brooding on his misfortunes—but she'd been blessed with her family. So blessed.

'My grandmother came to the rescue. She provided a roof over my head, sent me to school and made sure I had everything I needed. She was busy with her business interests and charity work, but she made what time she could for me. I'll be grateful to her forever. I love her dearly, but she's the "stiff upper lip and let's get on with it" type, if you know what I mean?'

The poor little boy that he'd been, though, would've craved a mother like hers. One who would smother him in hugs and love, making him feel secure and safe and the centre of the universe.

'But it only struck me this evening, when I was thinking about how you want to give your family a worry-free Christmas, that I've barely given my grandmother a second thought. And she deserves better from me. She must be terrified that I'll follow in the same path as my father and turn to drugs.' He met her gaze. 'Which I'm not, by the way.'

Thank heavens!

'But it's never crossed my mind to reassure her that I'm in no danger of doing any such thing.'

She reached out to squeeze his arm. 'But that's something you can fix. You don't need to sit here in the half-dark beating yourself up about it.'

He straightened. 'I can ring her tomorrow.'

'That's an excellent start. Though, in my experience, actions speak louder than words.'

His brows lowered and he pursed his lips. *Don't look at the lips!*

'You're right. She needs to see me doing things. Decorating the hall is a start. Telling her about my plans for the walled garden and the pipistrelles is another.' His nose curled. 'As would being seen in the village.'

She slapped her hands to her knees. 'Let's call that Plan A, shall we? We can both turn things around. And two heads are always better than one. Together we should be able to find a way forward and get back on track.' She groaned. 'And listen to me descending into cliché like some kind of motivational calendar. Enough with the brooding.' She stood. 'Cocoa?'

* * *

'What would you like to drink?'

Chloe glanced at the blackboard by the bar and her delectable lips stretched into a grin. 'Mulled wine, please. It's freezing outside and I want to find out if that stuff really does warm you up.'

He wasn't sure why, but it made him laugh. 'Go grab a seat by the fire and I'll get the drinks.'

She hesitated. 'What?' he demanded, instantly alert.

'Are you okay about being here tonight? There're more people in than I thought there'd be.'

Was she looking for a reason to leave? She hadn't been particularly enthusiastic when he'd suggested the outing. 'It's darts night, that's all. And I'm fine. Everyone here is a local. The tourists all go to The Royal Oak with its refurbished bar, fancy cocktails and even fancier cuisine.'

Without another word, she went to find a table.

'What do you think?' he asked a short while later.

'Of what, the wine or the pub?'

'Both.'

'The wine is…interesting.'

Uh huh. She hated it.

'And I'm in love with The Nag's Head.'

His head came up. She was?

'Oh, and by the way, I've entered us in the darts competition.'

He choked on his bitter. 'You've what?' He came here to be seen. Not to *participate*.

'You said it was darts night, so I figured that's what we were supposed to do. Also there's a Christmas ham up for grabs and I *really* want to win it.'

'You can play?'

'Doh! I have two older brothers. And I'm good.'

'I was *really* good when I was at university,' he shot back.

She raked him up and down with one unimpressed glance. 'How long ago was that? Last century? Come on, buster, we're heading for the practice board to see if we can get your eye in before the comp starts for real.'

He took a generous gulp of beer. 'Game on!'

Chloe was a hit with the other competitors, most of whom had known him since he was a boy. They didn't win the Christmas ham, but they did get third prize of a small Christmas pudding. He also filmed a snatch of video on his phone of Chloe, after her second drink—a pint of bitter— leading the crowd in a round of 'Kookaburra Sits in the Old Gum Tree'. Her mum would love it!

He couldn't remember the last time he'd had so much fun.

He frowned at that thought. Once Chloe's contract was completed, she'd be gone. Just as his parents had gone, and just as his job had gone.

Except, in this instance, Chloe didn't owe him anything.

Rely on nothing. Rely on nobody.

He could enjoy it while it lasted, but he couldn't get used to it. He'd help her find her Christmas mojo, she'd help him convince his grandmother he was fine, she'd create the garden of his dreams, and then they'd go their merry ways. Separately.

'So you're happy with all that then?'

Beau glanced around the garden and nodded. In his mind's eye he could see Chloe's vision for the garden come to life and it was even better than the one he'd imagined. They could turn this garden into a thriving sanctuary.

He should consider establishing some beehives too. Not in the walled garden, but maybe on the other side of the orchard. He'd completed a beekeeping course a few years ago. He suddenly saw that this garden could be the start of something bigger. He *ought* to dream bigger.

'Beau?'

He bumped back to find Chloe staring at him, a frown in the treacle-dark depths of her eyes. 'Sorry, what did you say?'

'You're happy with the proposed water feature? Large pond here, a little rill running either side to a fountain on one side and a pool on the other?'

'Absolutely. That was an inspired idea. I love it.'

She blinked, and he realised how miserly he'd been with his praise.

'You're confident that you, George and I can do all the necessary physical labour?'

'Absolutely.'

She swallowed, her hands twisting together. 'Just so you know, I'll be sourcing what I can locally—stone for the garden beds and paths, all the plants, as well as soil and fertiliser. You might as well generate what goodwill you can in the community.'

Her words warmed him. She'd put a lot of thought into this—was doing all she could to make things easy for him. 'Chloe, you've worked miracles here. I can't tell you how happy I am with everything you've proposed. And how grateful I am for your vision and all of your hard work.'

Her mouth fell open. She hauled it back into place, eyeing him carefully. 'I, um…excellent.' She rubbed a hand across her chest as if to dislodge an ache. 'I'm pleased you're so happy with what we're doing here and I wondered…'

He leaned towards her. 'Yes?'

'Look, Beau, would you consider letting me take before and after photos of the garden for my portfolio?'

Everything inside him snapped tight. 'Absolutely not!' How could she ask him such a thing? His hands clenched and he found himself breathing hard. 'It's out of the question. I thought I'd made that clear.' He'd thought they were on the same page. Realising they weren't cut him to the quick.

Before he could continue to rant, or turn on his heel and stalk off, she raised her hands. 'Okay, okay, keep your hair on. Just thought I'd ask.'

They stared at each other and he did what he could to unclench his jaw.

'So back to what we were talking about before.' She rushed back into speech. 'You're happy? There's nothing you want to add or subtract?'

He tried to get his breathing back under control, and refused to feel guilty for the dimming of the light in her eyes. 'Why? Do you feel there's something missing?'

'Not at all. But it doesn't matter what I think. What matters is making your vision real.'

What she thought *did* matter.

No, it doesn't.

Yes, it does.

Rolling his shoulders, he did what he could to dislodge the weight that wanted to settle over him. Instead he found himself caught in her stare, and those dark compelling eyes—

He dragged his gaze away. Her opinion mattered because she was the designer. That was all. 'I approve of all the suggestions you've made for the garden. You've not just captured what I wanted, but you've built on my original ideas and made them even better.'

'That's good to know.'

The vulnerability he saw in her face, before it was blinked away, caught at him. He wanted to swear and swear. 'I've been so selfishly caught up in myself I hadn't realised how parsimonious I've been with my praise.'

She started. 'Oh, I don't need praise. I just want to be sure I have everything exactly right before we start breaking serious ground.'

He stared at her, things inside him throbbing. 'Ever since I saw the photographs of the garden you won that award for I knew you were the right designer. When that was combined with your knowledge of English country gardens—'

He broke off with a frown. 'Why do you know so much about English country gardens?'

'I took it as an elective in my second year.' She shrugged. 'Blame *Wind in the Willows*, *The Secret Garden* and Beatrix Potter. They were firm favourites when I was growing up, and I was always a bit envious that I couldn't create a garden like that in Sydney.'

He gestured around. 'So why should you feel so anxious now about getting this right?'

Her nose wrinkled in a way that he found enchanting. Except she didn't do it to enchant him, he knew that. But then he was beginning to find a lot of things about Chloe enchanting.

You've been holed up on your own for too long. He shook the thought off. Once he had the garden to focus on, his life would begin to have a rhythm once more. It would start to feel full. He'd have a purpose.

'I haven't done much design work in the last two years.' She gave a hollow laugh that brought his focus immediately back to the here and now. 'Who am I kidding? I've not done *any* design work in the last two years.'

Not since her husband had died.

It didn't matter if Beau had scars that rendered him unrecognisable or was the most beautiful man in the world. Chloe didn't see him as a man. She'd never see him as a man. Her husband still filled her vision. He thought he'd known grief, but he hadn't known grief like that.

'How have you been making ends meet, then, Chloe?'

For some reason his words made her flinch, and he took an immediate step back. 'Sorry, that's none of my business. It's just…if I were in your shoes I think I'd want to lose myself in my job, try and find some solace in what I was good at.'

'Liar.' But the word carried no sting, and her eyes held no accusation. 'What did you do when your world came tumbling down? You holed up here like a bear with a sore head and bellowed at anyone who came near.'

He rubbed a hand over his face. 'I needed time to grieve before I could find a way forward.'

She glanced up, her eyes sharp. 'And this—'

she gestured at the garden '—is your way forward?'

It was.

'Mark and I went into business with his parents—a nursery-cum-garden-centre. After he died, I couldn't face dealing with other people so his parents took over all of the customer service, while I did a lot of the grunt work—the planting, mulching, raising seedlings.' She shrugged. 'I guess I'm just ready now to get back to my real work.'

He had a feeling that process hadn't been as seamless as she'd made it sound. He opened his mouth to probe further.

'You're confident the work we'll be doing won't disturb the pipistrelles?'

Clearly she didn't want to talk about it. He struggled with it for a moment and then let it go. It wasn't his place to probe. 'We're taking every precaution. Once we're done, this is going to be pipistrelle nirvana. I have big plans.'

Her eyes brightened, so he went on to explain how he was purchasing boxes to encourage more pipistrelles to the garden, the research he was doing on tracking devices so he could discover how far afield they went, and how he hoped the garden would—

'Hold on! Hold on!'

He bumped back to earth with a crash, grimaced. 'Sorry, that was probably way more information than you needed.' He'd just wanted to rid her eyes of their quiet desperation.

'No, it's fascinating.' She pulled her phone from her pocket. 'I mean *really* fascinating.'

She meant it, and against his better judgement his chest expanded.

'But you need to record this for your own records. It's gold!'

His head snapped back. 'You want to film me?' The thought had him wanting to yell and thunder, and then punch something.

She looked suddenly and gut-wrenchingly unsure of herself. 'Well, I just thought… I figured when you're writing your research up it'd be a useful record, a kind of diary.' She took a step back. 'Sorry, it was probably a stupid suggestion.'

He felt like a heel.

'Mum, Dad and my nephews loved that piece of video you took of me singing in the pub last night. So I probably just have videoing on my mind.' She sent him an apologetic smile. 'My mum thinks you're the bee's knees.'

He closed his eyes and counted to three. Before he could give himself too much time to think, he opened them again and said, 'Actually, it's a good idea.'

Her jaw dropped.

He winced.

'Sorry.' She dragged it back into place. 'I'm

just so used to saying the wrong thing around you that I thought this was another classic example.'

He shook his head, gritting his teeth. 'I just… it's a stupid thing to get hung up on.'

She opened her mouth and he waited for her to assure him it wasn't stupid at all. She didn't. She just shrugged. 'Then why don't you get un-hung-up about it? Let's do the video. If you hate it, you can always delete it and there'll be no harm done. And if you don't hate it, it'll then become part of your garden diary. And that's interesting in itself, don't you think?'

'Fine.' He refused to think too hard about any of it.

She started filming. 'Tell me what's so exciting about this garden, Beau.'

Without any conscious thought, he slipped immediately into documentary-making mode. He explained how the garden had been in his family for generations, but had been sadly neglected for the past decade. He described how he wanted to create a sanctuary for birds and butterflies and any other wildlife that found its way here.

He strolled down to the hornbeam tree and she followed, her phone trained on him the entire time. He described the unusual smell that had sent him investigating further. Then he took the phone and filmed the tiny bodies of the pipistrelles sleeping in their sheltered corner. He described what they were, how their habitats were being destroyed and how he hoped the garden would become a haven for them.

When he emerged back onto the path, he aimed the camera at Chloe, sitting on the low wall of a garden bed. 'Right, tit for tat. Tell me about the vision you have for this garden.'

Her eyes widened. She shot to her feet and wiped her hands on the seat of her trousers. 'Oh…um…' She made a couple of false starts, insisted they start at the other end of the garden where work was going to start first. And then she walked them through, stage by stage, what they were going to do and how it would all look when it was finished.

She met his gaze and shrugged. 'I think that's all from me.'

He clicked the off button, and they stood staring at each other. He handed the phone back to her, feeling numb. 'I've practically drained your battery.'

She shrugged as if that was no big deal. 'I'll put it on the charger when we go back to the house.'

Batteries could be recharged. She was right. It was no big deal.

'You were amazing.' She stared at him with huge eyes, held up her phone. 'You're a natural. You have such *presence*. You had me mesmerised.' She leaned towards him. 'How did it feel?'

Clearly she thought it'd felt good. Clearly she

expected him to feel as elated and exhilarated as she did. She couldn't be more wrong.

A numbness at his very centre had started to thaw, and he didn't want it to—he wanted to put it back to sleep, put it back on ice. But now that it'd started, it seemed there was nothing he could do to stop it. It felt as if his entire chest were caving in from the inside out.

His face twisted. Ugly words clawed at his throat.

She fell back, devastation spreading across her lovely face.

Turning on his heel, he left the garden before he did something, said something, he'd regret.

She didn't call him back, didn't run after him. He told himself he was glad, told himself that he wanted solitude.

He strode into the house and stormed straight to his study, not bothering to take his boots off first. He slammed the door to dispel some of his pent-up aggression, before slumping at his desk, head in hands.

All he could see when he closed his eyes was the expression on Chloe's face when she'd realised how the filming had made him feel.

When he opened them again, all he could feel was loss and pain. That innocuous piece of filming had brought home to him with a vengeance all that he'd lost. He'd thought he'd come to terms with the fact that the career he'd loved was gone forever. His harsh laugh reverberated in the air, mocking him.

His computer pinged to announce an incoming message. He lifted his head to glare at it. He had two messages—one from Chloe's mum and the other from his grandmother. He opened the one from Mrs Jennings first.

Dear Beau,
Thank you so much for taking Chloe out and making sure she enjoyed herself. It was kind of you to film what you did. It did my heart so much good. You're a kind boy.

He dragged a hand down his face. *Not* kind. Making Chloe feel responsible for the fact life hadn't panned out the way he'd wanted it to was the antithesis of kind. Nothing that had happened in the garden this afternoon had been her fault.

He turned to his grandmother's email.

Dear Recalcitrant Grandson of Mine,
I've barely spoken to you in two months. And before you contradict me, I don't consider email an adequate substitute.

The thought of you at Dawncarden alone this Christmas, without even Stephanie to keep you company, is intolerable. You keep assuring me you're fine, but I don't believe that for a moment.

Unless you can convince me otherwise I'm cancelling Christmas in Florence and descending to disturb your solitude.

Damn!

Another ping sounded. An email from Chloe. She sent no message just…

He swallowed. She'd sent him the video file.

He opened it, his heart thumping so hard it hurt. He watched the video all the way through and then turned it off with a savage stab of his finger and leaned back in his chair to glare at the ceiling.

Slamming back to his desk, he watched the video again, and frowned. It was undeniably amateur and yet he couldn't deny that he came across…*well*. Even given his scars. He spoke with assurance, and the video had captured his passion and enthusiasm.

Chloe was right. This would be an invaluable record.

He blinked, electrified for a moment, and then started frantically typing.

Dear Put-Upon-Though-Sainted Grandmother,

Apologies for my lack of communication. Put me in front of a camera and I can talk for hours, but ask me to pick up the phone and I can barely string two sentences together.

Let me assure you I'm well. The reason I've been so quiet is I'm immersed in my latest project—restoring the walled garden. Watch the piece of attached video and I believe you'll find that you can enjoy Florence with your mind at rest.

Your Recalcitrant-But-Ever-Loving-Grandson, Beau

He hit 'send' and leaned back. He even found one corner of his mouth lifting.

CHAPTER SIX

CHLOE BEAT THE shortbread mixture, wielding the wooden spoon like a hoe, putting her whole back into it. She pounded until her arm started to ache, and then she changed arms. She would not cry.

The expression on Beau's face when she'd asked him how he'd felt after that filming…

She flinched as it played through her mind for the hundredth time.

Oh, yes, you thought you had all the answers. Just get him to jump back in the saddle and all would be well, right?

She couldn't have been more wrong if she'd tried.

Dropping into a chair, she wished with everything inside her that she could start the day again, wished she could rethink her impulsive suggestion that he keep a video diary of the garden.

The outline of the table started to blur. It had seemed such a good idea at the time, but it had backfired spectacularly. And she'd do anything she could to spare Beau further pain. He didn't deserve it. He was dealing with enough.

She scrubbed a hand down her face. Somewhere during the last fortnight she'd started to like him. He didn't mind her losing her temper— in fact she was starting to think he encouraged it as if he knew she needed the outlet and was more than happy to be her figurative punching bag. Nobody had ever done that for her before.

Some of the hard knots of anger and ugliness simmering at the centre of her had started to lose their ferocity. That was all down to Beau.

He'd reminded her that there were still things in her life that she ought to be grateful for. Like her family. Not that she'd ever forgotten that, not really. But she could *feel* it again—feel the blessing of it in her heart. It mightn't sound like much, but it made all the difference in the world.

Footsteps sounded in the corridor leading to the kitchen and, as they could only belong to one person, she leapt to her feet and started beating the shortbread dough once again.

Could you pound the dough too much? She shrugged. These were either going to be really good or, um…not.

Her arm halted mid-pound, though, when Beau entered the kitchen. She had no hope of feigning busyness. Not when he looked at her like that. She opened her mouth to say something and then closed it again, lowered her arm. She didn't want to say something inane, but more to the point she didn't want to say anything that would hurt, trouble, perturb or disturb him in any way, shape, form or fashion.

She ached to find words that would comfort and encourage him instead. The thought made her blink. How long had it been since she hoped for something like that for someone else? When had her grief become so selfish?

'I want to apologise for my behaviour earlier.' Beau stared at the dough in the bowl, raked a hand through his hair. 'I was rude, and I expect my actions were baffling, and—'

'No!' The word shot out of her and his gaze speared to hers. Her heart started to pound though she didn't know why. 'No,' she said again, more measured this time. 'I'm the one who should be apologising. I pushed you to do something you didn't want to do. I thought it would be good for you. Ha!' She dumped the contents of the mixing bowl onto the table and started savagely flattening it with hard thumps of her palm.

He frowned and pointed. 'I uh—'

'As if I'm a therapist or something! But what do I know? I shouldn't have—' She broke off, realising he was pointing at the dough. She stared up at him and then down at the lump in front of her. 'What?'

He shook his head. 'It doesn't matter.'

She knew it didn't look like much at the moment, and she no doubt lacked Stephanie's flair, but just wait until she pulled it from the oven later. Mentally, she crossed her fingers.

She pulled her mind back to the conversation. 'I'm sorry, Beau. What I'm trying to say is that I've made enough of a mess of my own life. I've no right to be telling anyone else how they ought to be living.'

'I don't think your life is a mess.'

He didn't?

'I think you're remarkably talented with a bright future ahead of you.'

Her throat thickened. 'Thank you.'

He dropped into a chair. 'And you didn't force me to do that filming. Making a video diary is sensible. But once it was done, once we'd wrapped up...'

She abandoned the shortbread and sat too. It felt as if she ought to give him all of her attention. And she wanted to. She wanted to listen to him as much as he'd listened to her. But her eyes snagged on the breadth of those shoulders and the promise of the strength in that big powerful body and a pulse deep inside her quickened.

She did what she could to ignore it.

He lifted his head. 'It was so seamless, slipping back into character like that.'

He looked completely at a loss. It had clearly taken him off guard, and the glimpse of his vulnerability made her ache. 'Would you like to know what I think?'

She asked rather than rattling straight into speech and giving her opinion without thought. She had absolutely no intention of giving her opinion where it wasn't needed and making him feel twice as bad. She was through with being that person.

He met her gaze. 'Yes.'

It was just a simple word, but it carried weight. It reminded her that he'd told her he trusted her. And she wanted to be worthy of that trust. 'I don't think you were ever playing a part on your documentaries, so it's not that you slipped back into character, you just started sharing a deeper part of yourself again.'

He frowned.

She leaned towards him and his scent made her suddenly hungry—not for food, but for snow and sun and running and swimming. She eased back, doing what she could to crush her crazy imaginings. *Focus.* 'What I mean is, when you were on the television, you shared your passion for the natural world with your audience. You made us feel it too. You made us care.'

He stared. 'Is that how my documentaries really made you feel?'

She nodded, and then her hands suddenly clenched. 'And now the world is lesser because your stupid TV network dumped you and we no longer get your point of view on the airwaves. It sucks.'

One side of his mouth hooked up. 'You're very good for my ego, you know that?' But then his smile faded. 'That little piece of filming today brought home how much I miss making documentaries. I hate that I can no longer do that, that it's an option that's closed to me now.'

Was it closed to him, though? She had no idea how television worked. Were the networks really so superficial as to rate what a person looked like above their qualifications and expertise?

'I just watched the file you sent me.'

'And?'

'It was good.'

She could've told him that till she was blue in the face, but he wouldn't have believed her. She was glad he could recognise it for himself. 'So you're feeling okay again?'

'I forgot that not everything that hurts is bad for you.'

The words knocked the breath from her body.

'I think that's something you understand. Losing Mark has had a wealth of pain descending on your head.'

Her head, her heart, her life.

'But I don't think you'd give it back, because to not hurt would mean to not have loved him as much as you did.'

She couldn't speak so she simply nodded.

'Losing a job isn't anywhere near as bad as losing someone you love, but…'

With a superhuman effort she swallowed the lump in her throat. 'But you loved your job more than most people love their jobs. It wasn't just a job to you, but a calling.'

They stared at each other for a long time. His eyes had turned dark and his mouth pressed into a hard line as if holding back some strong emotion. 'Thank you,' he finally said. 'I knew you'd understand.'

And in that moment something arced between them and began to burn. He frowned. She frowned. And then he eased back in his seat and she leapt to her feet and started cutting circles of shortbread from the dough.

'It occurred to me that while I might not be able to make documentaries on a large scale any more, I can make them for myself. There's absolutely no reason why I can't keep my own ongoing video diary of the garden. It's going to be fascinating to see how it grows and develops, what it attracts and what comes to live there. I've been focussed on the more exotic picture for so long because it draws an audience, but what happens here in our own backyards is every bit as important.'

But who would get to see those videos? Who would benefit from all of his insight and knowledge? She'd pay good money to watch them and hear his thoughts.

'Can I ask something?'

'Sure?' But a wary light entered his eyes.

'Look, you can tell me to shut up if you want. I won't be offended. It's just I have no idea how TV works.'

'What do you want to know?'

'There's more than one network, right? Just because one network dumped you doesn't mean another one wouldn't want you.' She frowned. 'Or does it?'

He didn't answer immediately, and she spread parchment paper onto a baking tray to appear busy and give him some space, and tried to lift the first of her shortbread circles from the table. It refused to budge. Grabbing a butter knife, she tried to slide it beneath the circle and promptly mashed it.

She glanced up to find Beau trying not to laugh. She spread her hands. She thought she'd followed Stephanie's recipe to the letter. She might've been a little energetic with the beating but…

'Stephanie sprinkles flour on the surface before rolling the dough out.'

She grimaced. 'A rookie mistake.'

'Here, give me a sharp knife and I'll be able to get these up for you.'

She sat while he did it. Each circle left a trace of dough behind. She'd need to scour the table to get it off.

'The networks are all chasing the next big thing.'

She snapped back to attention.

'All that matters in TV land are the ratings. And prior to *the incident* I was ranking number one.'

The incident being his run-in with that leopard.

She moistened suddenly dry lips. 'What actually happened, Beau?'

He was silent for a moment, didn't meet her eyes. 'Surely you've read the news reports.'

'They were hard to avoid at the time,' she acknowledged, 'but I never liked the sensationalism. Other than the fact that you were recovering, and I was pleased about that, I can't say I paid a whole lot of attention.' Her lips twisted. She'd been too focussed on her own grief to pay much attention to anyone else.

He set the last circle to the prepared tray and then sat in the chair she'd previously vacated. Instead of the entire length of the table resting between them, they now sat at right angles. She had an insane urge to reach out and trace the muscles in his forearm. She could imagine the living strength of his flesh and sinew and—

'The full story never made it to the papers anyway.'

She snapped back.

'We were filming in Africa, and we'd been following the leopard for a few weeks. We'd been getting some excellent footage, but I wanted to get a close-up.'

'Weren't you afraid? I mean, I know they're absolutely gobsmackingly beautiful, but I'd be afraid to get too close.'

'There's always an element of danger, of course, but we were careful. We knew she'd just eaten, and we hadn't presented any kind of threat to her in the weeks we'd been following her. So we set up and started the filming. I kept my voice low and my body still and unthreatening. All of us were enthralled. The light was perfect, we were getting great shots.'

He broke off and was quiet for a long moment. She swallowed. 'What went wrong?'

He glanced up, his eyes shadowed. 'One of the cameramen…' He turned more fully towards her. 'There's this thing that can happen when you stare at something through a lens. You start to feel removed from it—like you're watching it on your TV set in your living room. He'd become mesmerised. That leopard, she was one of the most beautiful things he'd ever seen and he kept moving closer and closer towards her.'

Her heart lurched into her throat.

'Too close. She felt threatened. We were on her turf and rather than flee, she wanted to protect it. I told him to back off, but it was too late.'

Perspiration broke out on her top lip. 'Beau?'

'It was my fault we were that close in the first place so I did the only thing I could think of. I distracted her.'

Her hands flew to her mouth. She dragged them away, suddenly and irrationally angry. 'You could've been killed! What were you thinking?'

'I didn't want to be responsible for someone else's death. The thought of that was worse than—' he shrugged '—anything.'

'But you could've been killed,' she repeated.

'Is that thought really so bad, Chloe?' he asked gently. 'People die every day.'

'Of course it's that bad! It's an awful thought, Beau. Just...*awful.*'

'You loved my documentary series, that much?'

'No! I mean, of course I loved it but the thought of you not being here...' She shook her head. 'If it'd happened back then before I knew you, well... I'd have been sad in the way people are sad when someone dies before their time. But now that I know you, the thought of you being dead is one of the worst thoughts in the world!'

The mixture of sincerity and horror in Chloe's eyes pierced Beau to his very centre. His heart pounded and his eyes stung. He leaned towards her. 'Why?'

Confusion raced across her features, along with consternation. And anger. Those eyebrows grew suddenly fierce. 'I feel that we understand each other. I feel that we're friends. And maybe you don't feel the same way. And maybe you don't know how rare it is, but—'

'I feel the same way.' The words were out of his mouth before he could help it. But he couldn't let her be the only vulnerable one here. Besides, it was the truth.

Her breath gave a funny little hitch. 'And maybe it isn't rare, this feeling.' She gestured between them. 'Maybe it's just that I haven't found it with anyone else because I've been indulging my grief for too long and since then I've been too busy putting on a happy face for everyone. But I don't have to pretend anything to you, and it feels...'

His heart hovered between heartbeats as if it didn't know whether to crash and burn or set sail. 'It feels?'

She shrugged, her eyes a little wild. 'Like heaven,' she hiccupped.

Which was exactly how he felt knowing she didn't care one jot about his scars.

He stared into those dark compelling eyes, and he felt seen, truly seen. Better still, he knew she did too and it was strangely freeing. Neither one of them wanted to hide.

And then she was in his arms and he didn't know if he'd moved first or if she had, but their lips met with a firm warmth that was neither rushed nor urgent, but irresistible for all that. He shaped his mouth to hers, and something warm brushed across the surface of his skin like a spring breeze, and the scent of lavender rose up all around him. Some hard thing inside him dissolved, replaced with light and warmth.

But when her lips opened beneath his, when her tongue tentatively touched his, that warmth became an all-consuming heat. Her body pressed full length against his and everything inside him raged with the need to possess this woman—to strip her of her clothes and explore every inch of her body, to learn all of its secrets. He wanted to drive her crazy with need until she begged for release.

Her hand snaked beneath his shirt and the skin-on-skin contact had him sucking in a breath. He wanted to feel all of her against all of him. Her head fell back when he pressed a series of kisses along her jawline, her fingers digging into him as if to keep herself anchored, their latent urgency urging him on, until he'd worked his way down to push aside the neckline of her shirt to take the hard bud of one nipple into his mouth through the thin material of her bra.

Her cry rang in his ears, and with a mad growl he pulled her shirt over her head before turning his full attention to her other breast. The sound of his name ripping from her throat, hoarse with desire, nearly undid him. In one fluid movement, he lifted her to the table and moved in between her thighs, pulling her hard up against him.

She flung her head back, her legs encircling his waist as if she had no intention of ever letting him go. Clamping her hands either side of his face, she pulled him down for another drugging kiss, her fingers idly tracing his scars, but it didn't spook him. She touched him the same way he touched her. As if she wanted to learn and memorise everything about him.

He wanted to sweep everything from the table, lay her back and bury himself inside her. Her arms around his neck, urgent, her lips parted with anticipation as if she couldn't get enough, her eyes desire-glazed as they met his...

I feel that we understand each other. I feel that we're friends.'

Her words replayed through his mind and he dragged in a ragged breath, forced himself to slow down...forced himself to meet those treacle-dark eyes. He wanted to be the friend she needed. He *needed* to be that friend. 'You're beautiful, Chloe.'

She blinked and swallowed, her eyes becoming suspiciously bright.

'And I can't tell you how much I want this—to make love with you. I ache with how much I want you.' With a gentle hand, he pushed the hair that had worked its way free from her braid back from her face. 'But I need to know that you want it too. I don't want you crying with remorse afterwards and I don't want you beating yourself up with regrets.' His chest hollowed out at the thought. 'I don't want to be that man for you.'

He watched, barely able to breathe, as comprehension dawned in her eyes.

'But if you do want this as much as I do—' he couldn't stop his hands from tightening fractionally on her waist '—I can promise you pleasure and release and orgasms that will rock your world.'

'Oh!' She gave a funny little hiccup and he sensed the war raging inside her.

He didn't want to, but he moved back, bringing her with him until they stood once again, both of their feet firmly planted on the floor. Picking up her shirt from where he'd thrown it to the chair behind, he handed it to her.

'You want me to get dressed?' she blurted out. *What are you doing? Kiss her again.*

'No.' He clenched his hands to fists. 'I want to do the caveman thing and tear the clothes from your body and ravish you.'

Her eyes grew so wide a man could fall into them.

'But instinct tells me you need some space.' He did what he could to temper the impatience roaring through him, the raging need. 'You said we understood each other. You said we were friends. And I think we are and I think we do.'

She frowned. 'You don't think I want you?'

'No, sweetheart, I know that you do.'

She gulped and reefed her shirt back on over her head, but her arms got tangled and he had to reach out and help her. Every touch was torture.

He forced himself back a step. 'Would you regret it if we made love?'

She lowered herself to the nearest chair, her lips trembling. 'I don't know.'

He made tea.

'I know I shouldn't feel guilty about making love with someone who isn't Mark.' She blew on her tea. 'In my head, I know there's nothing to feel guilty about.'

'But it's not how you feel here—' he touched a hand to his chest '—where it counts.'

She stared at him with a helplessness that speared into him. 'I'm sorry. I shouldn't have kissed you if I didn't know—'

'Rubbish.' He dismissed that with a single wave of his hand. 'We're adults, Chloe, not teenagers. *Consenting* adults,' he stressed. 'That consent can be withdrawn by either of us at any time.'

She stilled. 'That's true.'

An entirely different thought struck him. 'Have you ever had sex just for fun?'

Her cup halted halfway to her mouth. 'Sort of,' she said carefully.

'What does that mean?'

Her shoulders sagged. 'I've never had sex outside a committed relationship, if that's what you're asking.'

'Do you have a moral stance on it?' Maybe she was the kind of woman who equated sex with love. The thought had him choking. If she did, then he'd just had a lucky escape.

'I've never had a one-night stand or a friends-with-benefits arrangement or...' She set her tea down with a frown. 'Why on earth not? Most women my age have.'

He doubted it was due to a lack of opportunity. There was something vibrant and compelling about Chloe that even if she hadn't been so attractive would've drawn men to her.

'I guess I never found anyone tempting enough to throw that kind of caution to the wind.'

Her gaze flicked to him and darted away again, and he heard what she didn't say. *Until now.* She found *him* tempting. The thought had everything inside him growing hard and tight.

'How old were you when you met Mark?'

'We met at university. I was doing a Horticulture degree and he was doing Business. We didn't actually meet on campus, but we both worked at a garden centre during the holidays and on weekends.' One slim shoulder lifted. 'I was twenty when we started dating. I mean, we didn't get married until we were twenty-four, but we were committed from the beginning.'

'So you didn't actually have much of an opportunity to explore the sex-for-fun thing.'

'I guess not.'

He leaned close enough to feel the heat radiating off her body. 'Well, just so you know. If you decide you want to explore the sex-for-fun thing now, I'd make the perfect person to do that with.'

Her breath hitched and her pupils dilated, and he moved back, cleared the teapot and rinsed his mug. He wouldn't crowd her, and he wouldn't pressure her.

But he was damned if he wouldn't plant the seed of temptation firmly in her mind before he walked away.

He started for the door. 'Time to get back to work.'

She shot to her feet. 'What? Just like that?'

He closed his eyes and counted to three before turning around. 'Do you have an answer to my earlier question? Can you make love with me without regret or remorse?'

That same helpless indecision flashed through her eyes and he nodded. 'When you can answer that question with a yes then we have something to talk about. I don't want to be anyone's regret.'

Liar, an inner voice said as he walked away. If she threw herself at him now, threw caution to the wind, he'd be helpless to resist her. Lucky for both of them then that she didn't chase after him and throw caution to the wind.

Except it didn't feel lucky.

He closed his study door and leaned back against it, tried to catch his breath. Perhaps what had happened in the kitchen shouldn't have taken him off guard, but it had. The intensity and the need had shaken him to his foundations.

Maybe it was the sheer honesty between them—the initial snarling at one another that had given way to understanding that was now turning into friendship. Whatever was between them, though, it was only temporary. He knew that in his bones. Their lives were on very different trajectories, and, while he might have started to see that he didn't necessarily need to live like a monk, he wasn't giving up his solitude for anyone.

But it didn't mean they couldn't help each other in the meantime. Or find release in one another. Mark had been dead for two years. For two years it was clear that her grief had overshadowed everything else. But some instinct told him she was finally starting to come out the other side, and that she was ready to explore a physical relationship with a man again.

His heart pounded at the thought, and then he stilled as the suspicion that had been niggling at him for days finally crystallised. Why now, *in particular*, was it important for Chloe to put a front on for her family? Didn't the fact that she was designing gardens again prove that she was finally moving on with her life? Was she really worried she'd fall apart again this Christmas, or was there something more?

He moved across to his desk and tapped his fingers against the wood, and then he picked up his mobile and rang the house number.

'Dawncarden Court.'

'It's the tree-lighting ceremony in the village tonight,' he said without preamble. 'Interested? It'll provide us with another photo opportunity for your family. Also, my grandmother emailed earlier. She's worried about me and is threatening to change her plans and spend Christmas here after all, and I don't want her doing that. I sent her the piece of video you took of me earlier to explain why I've been so busy. But if I'm seen out and about in the village, hopefully one of her spies will report back.'

'You rang to tell me this rather than walked the length of the hall like an ordinary person?'

'Yep.' He didn't bother telling her he'd thought it wise for the two of them to cool down before they clapped eyes on each other again. 'You have a problem with that?'

'Seriously?'

Her outrage made his lips twitch. 'There's a reason Stephanie calls me lord and master.'

'Clearly!' she huffed, but he could tell from her voice that she was trying not to laugh.

'So do you want to go?'

She was quiet for several long moments. 'Okay,' she finally said. 'I've never been to a tree lighting. It'll be something fun to tell my folks about.'

'Don't bother with dinner, we'll grab something in the village.' And then he replaced the receiver before he said something he'd regret. Like, *Let's make love.*

A moment later he heard stomping at the far end of the corridor. 'It's polite to say goodbye before hanging up!' she hollered down the hallway.

'Oh, and by the way, I burned the shortbread. So bad luck if you were hoping for a piece of it.'

And then she stomped away again and he found himself grinning like an idiot.

CHAPTER SEVEN

CHLOE HUDDLED INTO the extra warm scarf Beau had loaned her. She'd wound it around her neck twice and it still covered her from chin to chest, the tails of the scarf angling beneath her coat to cover her breasts. The thought of chests and breasts, though, had her recalling the broad, lean strength of Beau's chest under her hands earlier. And when he'd touched her breasts…

Her lungs cramped and it was hard to breathe. Closing her eyes, she did what she could to unclench herself.

Thank God he'd given her time to think.

Thank God he'd kept his wits about him.

If he hadn't they'd have made love and… She swallowed. It would've been a mistake.

Are you sure about that?

Of course she was! It—

She bit back a groan. She ached with need. She wanted Beau so badly it had become a physical pain and she couldn't think of anything else. Didn't want to think of anything else.

She ought to be thinking about Mark!

Why? some inner demon demanded.

She choked on her glühwein. He'd been her *husband*. She'd loved him!

Had been. Had loved. Past tense, Chlo.

For the first time, rather than tear her apart, that realisation simply made her sad.

'Too strong?' Beau asked, nodding towards her environmentally friendly cardboard cup.

The stall vendor had told her that once he'd watched Beau's first documentary about the impact of plastics and global warming on the natural world, he'd immediately moved to more environmentally friendly products. In fact, the whole village had. They were so proud of him. She didn't think he realised just how much.

'Would you like me to get you something else instead? Hot chocolate?'

Her head lifted. 'Hot chocolate?'

'Made with the finest Dutch chocolate on real milk.'

Oh, my God, that sounded delicious—perfect, sweet…comforting.

He laughed at whatever he saw in her face. Moving to a nearby stall, he returned moments later with a steaming mug of hot chocolate.

She buried her nose in the fragrant steam, glancing everywhere but at him. Coloured lights hung from the shops that surrounded the village green and the scent of cinnamon and gingerbread filled the air. She pulled the fragrance into her lungs. 'The village looks pretty.'

'It really does.'

His frown had her eyebrows lifting. 'Why the surprise?'

'I don't know. I just…forgot.' He shook his head, his frown deepening. 'I'm coming to the sobering realisation that maybe I've been focussing too much on the ugliness of life rather than its beauty.'

The admission speared into her.

'Once upon a time I always noticed the beauty. I could see beneath any surface ugliness to what was hidden below. Deserts and mudflats aren't necessarily beautiful, but the life they contain…'

'The fact that life can exist in such harsh or strange places, there's beauty in that.'

'Exactly.' He gestured around. 'But one doesn't need to dig deep to find the beauty here in Ballingsmallard. The stone houses, the pretty lights. And nearby Exmoor is stunning.'

She'd read about Exmoor National Park and had every intention of visiting. 'When was the last time you had a ramble there?'

He didn't answer and she knew he hadn't been to Exmoor since his accident, even though it was practically on his doorstep.

He gestured. 'Looks like the ceremony is about to start.'

Three dignitaries mounted a temporary stage in front of the giant tree at the centre of the green. She sipped her hot chocolate and tried to focus on the festive message that the mayoress gave, but she was too aware of Beau—of his heat and latent power and how her body responded to every minute movement he made.

She straightened, though, when the tree lit up in a riot of colour. It was so pretty! Then the church choir sang 'Silent Night' and a lump lodged in her throat. She found herself leaning into Beau, needing the comfort of a friend in the same way she'd needed the comfort of the hot chocolate.

She was grateful when he didn't say anything, just put his arm around her shoulders and drew her against the warmth of his side. There was nothing suggestive or sexualised about the act. It was comfort and friendship. Nothing more.

But you want it to be more.

She ignored that. When the choir broke into a joyful rendition of 'Hark! The Herald Angels Sing' something inside her felt suddenly lighter.

'Okay, quick,' she ordered, moving out of his arms. 'You have to capture this on video.'

He snapped immediately into action and she could've hugged him.

He recorded a short video of her telling her family all about the tree lighting, extolling the virtues of hot chocolate, and then she pointed towards one of the nearby food vendors. 'I have no idea what that vendor is cooking, but it looks intriguing. As long as it's not something disgusting like snails or puppy dogs' tails, I'm going to try it.'

'Roasted chestnuts,' Beau said.

'Roasted chestnuts? Sounds delicious! I'll let

you all know what I think in my next email. Love
to everyone! I miss you all.' She blew a kiss to the
camera and Beau sent her a thumbs up.

'That was great. You're a natural.'

He was the natural. She was just chatting to her
family, and that was a piece of cake. There was no
way she could speak to a camera knowing thou-
sands of strangers were watching. Beau was the
one with real talent, and a part of her wept that
all of that talent and passion was going to waste.

'You're doing a great job, you know, Chloe.'

She snapped back.

'This is going to assure your family that all is
well.'

Actually, the smiling and acting happy hadn't
been as hard as she'd thought it would be. The
thought made her frown, but she shook it off and
followed Beau to the roasted chestnut stall.

'Can I ask you something?' he asked a little
while later when they were munching on roasted
chestnuts.

Which, by the way, were *truly* delicious. She
glanced up. 'Sure.'

'It's personal,' he warned.

She spluttered a laugh, even as things inside her
tightened. 'Of course it is. I'm not sure we know
any other way to be with each other.'

That utterly divine and perfect mouth firmed…
gentled…and then smiled. 'You could be right.'

She dragged her gaze from his mouth. 'Your question?'

He popped a chestnut in his mouth and chewed thoughtfully. 'I understand why your first Christmas without Mark was devastating. And I understand why the second one was too, marking as it did the anniversary of his death and knocking you for six again.'

She waited for the bone-crushing tension and weight of her grief to crush her, as it always did whenever she spoke about how lost she'd been without Mark during those first two Christmases, and kept waiting. Oh, there was the weight of sadness, but it wasn't crippling. Not as it had once been.

An awful thought struck her. Had her anger extinguished it? Anger that he'd taken out the second mortgage without telling her? That anger had been directed at herself just as much as it had been at him, though. She didn't want anger to be the lasting legacy left between them.

She halted and forced herself to bring his face to mind. It didn't make her flinch. It didn't make her want to cry…or to rail and rage. Was that a loss or a blessing?

'Chloe?'

She glanced up into summer-sea eyes. 'I don't miss him the way I used to. I feel bad about that.'

'It's to be expected,' he said gently. 'It's been two years. You've been forced to live without him, been forced to move on whether you liked it or not. It doesn't make you a bad person.'

'We promised each other forever.'

He took both bags of chestnuts and pushed them into the pockets of his coat before seizing her hands. 'Chloe, the two of you were hoping for forever, but you promised *till death do us part.*'

His words should've made her flinch, but they didn't.

'Would he want you to grieve him forever?'

'Of course not.' Nobody wanted that for the people they loved. They'd want them to move on and be happy.

'I feel like somewhere along the line I moved on and said goodbye without even realising it,' she blurted out. 'It feels wrong. Surely it should've been marked by some grand event or...'

She couldn't continue as tears clogged her throat and she found herself engulfed in Beau's cool, rich scent as strong arms went around her and pulled her to his chest. After a moment's hesitation she wrapped her arms around his waist and held on and tried to focus on her breathing. Holding onto Beau made her feel anchored as the panic and confusion pounded at her. For as long as she held onto him, it felt as though the badness couldn't overwhelm her. And like a storm blowing itself out, the guilt and regret slowly bled away.

She bumped back to earth, aware of people milling nearby and casting curious glances in their direction. Heavens, she was drawing attention to them and that was the one thing Beau hated.

She eased away and sent him a shaky smile. 'Sorry.'

He shook his head, those eyes searching her face. 'Nothing to apologise for. You okay?'

'Strangely enough, I am.' She laughed and pushed her hair back behind her ear, tried to appear perfectly normal.

Except being so close to him had ignited that latent demon inside her—the one that wanted her to drag Beau back home to his grand manor house, tear his clothes off and make wild, uninhibited love with him *just for fun*. And as soon as the notion lodged in her brain, a part of her demanded to know why that couldn't happen.

Because she'd be filled with regret and remorse afterwards.

No, you won't.

The denial rang through her, making her blink…making her stand taller.

'Hungry?' Beau asked. 'Did you want to go across to the pub for something more substantial than chestnuts?' He glanced down and stilled at whatever it was he saw in her eyes.

'I'm hungry, but not for food.' She kept her voice low. She didn't want anyone overhearing their conversation. 'Can I ask you a question?'

'I haven't asked mine yet.'

That made her blink. 'Okay, well, ask it.'

'I think I'd rather hear yours.'

Desire had flared to life in his eyes and it made her knees weak. Nobody had made her knees weak before. She'd had butterflies, happy shivers, and that sense of free-fall floating before, but not weak knees. All of them assailed her now.

She gripped the tails of her scarf in an effort to stop from throwing herself into his arms and making a spectacle of them both. She moved into the deeper shadows, away from the enormous lighted Christmas tree and food vendors, and he followed.

'You said that if I wanted to have sex just for fun that you would be the perfect person to do that with.' His quick intake of breath sounded loud in the quiet and shadows and an ache started up at the centre of her. 'What does that mean? That you've a lot of experience with that kind of thing?'

'I've had some experience,' he said carefully, 'but that's not what I meant. Your life isn't here in England, but mine is. If you and I are the proverbial ships passing in the night then Dawncarden is merely the harbour you've docked in for the next couple of months. If we were to become lovers, Chloe, there'd be no expectations. We both know you're leaving at the end of your contract, and whatever happens between us is temporary. There's something freeing about that, don't you think?'

She nodded slowly. 'It makes me feel…uninhibited.' She shivered, but not from the cold. Beneath her layers of clothes her nipples beaded.

'You can explore a part of yourself you never have before.'

'And what about you? What do you get?'

He moved in so close she could feel his breath on her cheek. 'I get to make love with a woman who has bewitched me from the moment she introduced herself as Chloe Ivy Belle Jennings. I get to feel alive again in a way I never thought I would. I get to...not hide.'

That last admission punched the breath from her body. He didn't need to hide. Not from her.

'Beau?'

'Yes?'

'Can we go back to Dawncarden *now*?'

He didn't answer. He just grabbed her hand and started for the car.

The moment they burst through the back door and into the warmth of the kitchen, Chloe seized Beau's face in her hands and kissed him, open-mouthed and hungry. He answered her hunger with his own. Thrusting a hand in her hair, he cradled her skull, angling her head until he could ravish her mouth, raking her need until his name was dragged from her throat.

She needed him now!

He glanced at the kitchen table. 'I've had dreams about stretching you out on that table and doing things to your body until you're screaming for a release, but tonight at least I need to pretend to be a gentleman rather than a caveman and—'

'To hell with that!' She was tugging off her boots and socks and leaving them where they fell and dropping her coat to the floor. 'I don't want a gentleman. I want you, Beau.'

She hauled her jumper over her head, taking the long-sleeved T-shirt with it. Her hands went to the waistband of her jeans, but he moved in close, his hands clamping over hers, and that weak-kneed, tummy-fluttering thing swamped her.

'Are you sure about this?'

She nodded. 'I'm sure, Beau. Very sure. I want you *now*.'

It was a cry from her soul and he answered it with a deep drugging kiss. All she could do was wrap her arms around his shoulders and hold on tight.

He divested her of her jeans and panties, her bra, and she'd managed to drag his jumper over his head, but then his hands were on her nakedness, doing things to her that made her breath catch and gasp and sending her mindless with desire and need.

Lifting her, he laid her on the table with a gentleness that had a lump forming in her throat. His eyes glittered as he stared down at her. She had a feeling she ought to feel self-conscious, but she didn't. The approval and fire in his eyes were all that she needed. She wanted to be wanton for him, to prove that he was virile and beautiful despite his scars.

'You are beautiful,' he said, his voice hoarse.

'And you're wearing too many clothes,' she said, her voice just as husky.

That glorious mouth hooked up. 'You have no idea the kind of lustful thoughts I've had about you and this table.'

'Then let's put them into action,' she said, feeling bold as the demands of her body for release overcame any veneer of either politeness or composure.

'Oh, I'm planning to, sweetheart, don't have any doubt about that.'

Seizing her legs beneath her thighs, he pulled her down the table until she was flush against the hardness in his jeans. Stars burst behind her eyelids.

'You need to be naked,' she started to croak, but he leaned down instead and took one beaded nipple into his mouth and grazed it gently with his teeth, his hands resting firmly on her shoulders to keep her in place, and nothing had ever felt hotter in her life.

Beau explored every inch of Chloe's body and revelled in the scent, feel and taste of her. Her gasps and moans urging him on. This moment, now, marked a new beginning for her, and he wanted to help her mark that milestone with fireworks and fun. And no regrets. It was that knowledge that helped him keep his rampaging desires in check and to focus wholly on her.

Settling between her thighs, he loved her with his mouth and tongue, his hands firm on her hips to keep her still as he concentrated on bringing her to the brink of orgasm and holding her there in the throes of imminent pleasure before hurtling her over the edge. Her cries rang in his ears, making something in him lift and dance. He rested his cheek lightly on her stomach as he waited for her to descend back to earth.

He didn't move until he felt her hands flutter, and then he glanced up to find her eyes had filled with tears.

'Oh, sweetheart.' His gut clenched and for some absurd reason his throat thickened, his eyes stinging too in sympathy. 'You promised me you wouldn't cry.'

Before he could pull her into the shelter of his arms, where he wished he could wipe away all her pain, she sat up, her hands going either side of his face, and she shook her head. 'Not sad, not regretful—happy tears.' And then she pulled him in for a kiss so full of warmth and joy he felt as if he were wrapped in a blanket in front of a roaring fire with a myriad woodland animals cavorting around him.

Oh, for God's sake, get a grip.

She rested her forehead against his. 'Thank you, Beau. Just…thank you.'

She made him feel like a superhero, as if he were capable of anything and everything; that he was the best lover that had ever lived. 'Any time,' he said with a grin, and he meant it.

'So…' She eased back and moistened her lips, her eyes going so dark they were almost black. 'You've played out your fantasy. Does that mean I can play out mine now?'

She could have whatever she damn well pleased 'What's your fantasy?'

'Getting you naked and straddling you in that chair.' She nodded at the nearest kitchen chair. His groin, his throat, his very skin tightened until he thought he'd burst. 'Condoms are in my bedside drawer,' was all he could manage to croak.

'My fantasy just changed to straddling you in your bed.'

Her breath had grown shallow and uneven and if he could've, he'd have laughed at the speed of her reply. Instead he lifted her in his arms and strode through the baronial hall, up the staircase, and down the corridor to his bedroom.

They shucked his clothes with more speed than grace and then she pushed him back onto the bed and he submitted. She clearly wanted to be in charge and he wanted her to have everything she wanted.

'I don't want to wait,' she whispered.

He nodded to tell her that was fine by him, unable to get words out through clenched teeth as she sheathed him with a condom. Her hands on his body set off electric charges. Then she lowered herself onto him with an impatience that he found edifying but it pushed him immediately to the edges of his limits.

Dear God! She felt warm and soft and perfect and the way her body gripped him had him throwing his head back with a low growl.

She stilled. His eyes flew to hers and he found her staring at him, eyes as huge as an owl's. He took her hands, lifted them to his mouth. 'Is everything okay? If you want to stop, Chloe, that *is* okay.' He gritted his teeth and it took all of his strength to not move. It would be okay. It was her prerogative. He would behave like a gentleman, not a caveman.

'I don't want to stop.'

He gazed heavenward. 'Thank you, God,' he whispered.

'It's just…you feel perfect.'

She moved up and down tentatively, making him grip the sheets in his hands. 'So do you,' he ground out.

'*Really* perfect.'

He realised she was right. Had he ever felt so in tune with someone so immediately? He started to frown, but then she moved with a calculated intent and a growing passion that he was powerless to resist. He didn't want to resist. It flung him out of himself and had him hurtling towards the stars. When her body clenched around his as she climaxed, he followed with a loud cry that felt wrenched from the very depths of his soul. A cry that left him feeling clean and whole...and happy.

He pulled her close into his side, and they lay there with closed eyes, relishing the warm hum of their bodies. And it was a long time before either one of them returned back to earth and reason.

They made love again later that night, and then again in the morning when they showered together. As they lay in his king-size bed, her fingers lightly playing across his chest as his brushed up and down her spine in light lazy strokes, he wanted the moment to last forever.

'So...' She rested her chin on his chest and glanced up at him, her lips curving into a smile that had him itching to kiss her again. 'What was the question you were going to ask me last night? The *personal* question?'

Ah...

She frowned and eased away. 'Is it something awful?'

He smoothed out her brow with his finger. 'I don't think so. If it is, then just say so and we'll forget about it.'

'Okay, spill.'

'I just wondered why, when you haven't put on a

front for your family for the last two Christmases, why you're doing so this Christmas.'

Her lips immediately drooped and he mentally kicked himself for asking. He should've saved it for another time. Or not asked about it at all. She rested her head on his shoulder and he could no longer see her face. 'We don't have to talk about it, Chloe. Not if you don't want to.'

'It's okay. I feel as if I could tell you anything and you wouldn't tell another soul.'

Her words shorted his breath. He had to swallow before he could speak. 'I know what it's like to feel exposed. I'd never reveal your secrets, even if I didn't agree with them.'

'Ditto,' she murmured, her breath a soft brush of warmth on his chest.

She was quiet for a long moment, before pulling in a deep breath. 'I told you how devastated I was after Mark died and how I lost interest in everything. I did the physical work required of me at the garden centre, but I was moving through a thick fog and mentally not present most of the time.'

His arm tightened about her. He wished she'd been spared such pain.

'Earlier this year, I started to come out of that fog, much to everyone's relief.'

'You'd started to turn your face to the future. You shouldn't feel guilty about that, Chloe.'

She nodded, but it was more an absent acknowledgement than a heartfelt acceptance. 'It meant that Mark's parents finally felt able to tell me the dire straits the business had been in.'

He stiffened.

She eased away and they both sat up against the pillows. 'They'd been trying to protect me but could no longer keep the truth from me. Without my knowledge, Mark had taken out a second mortgage on our house to help keep the business afloat. And the bank was threatening to foreclose.'

Hell!

'And then I got so damn angry—at Mark for doing that without discussing it with me first, with my in-laws for keeping me in the dark for so long, though I know they were only trying to protect me, but mostly with myself for taking so long to care about anything else beyond my own grief when I could've been doing something to help turn things around.'

'I'm sorry, Chloe.' Would she accept a loan from him? Whether the answer was a yes or a no, instinct told him now wouldn't be the right time to make the offer.

'But, Beau, I've put *my* family through enough. They loved Mark. I didn't want to burden them with any further woes.'

His heart burned. She'd been dealing with this all alone?

'But I knew I'd never be able to get through Christmas convincingly enough for them, and my mother…' She blew out a breath, looking deliciously rumpled and sexy. 'Well, you've met her. She can be like a dog with a bone once she senses something is wrong. Besides, I want to fix the problem on my own, and I don't want them offering to go into debt to bail me out. I'm not letting them do that.' She met his gaze. 'They deserve to enjoy this Christmas unmarred by my dramas.'

He didn't know if he agreed with that or not, but he couldn't deny that her actions were pure. She loved her family. She wanted only good things for them. And she wanted to protect their memory of Mark. But... He dragged in a breath. 'Are you, though?'

'Am I what?'

'Fixing the problem.'

She gnawed on her bottom lip. 'The commission you've paid me so far has giving me breathing space as far as the house goes.'

But she probably needed another contract like this one, maybe two, to get back on her feet properly. She probably needed to keep the money rolling in and—

Beau slapped a hand to his brow. 'That's why you asked if you could take photos of my garden for your portfolio!'

'But I totally see your point,' she said, neither confirming nor denying the claim. 'The garden is going to be your haven. I understand why you don't want to share it with anyone.'

She made him sound like some kind of self-ish recluse!

'I respect that, Beau.'

He went back over all the things she'd said and all that he knew about her and frowned.

She sat up straighter. 'What?'

'We need coffee and toast and bacon.'

'You want to build me up before slugging me with more reality?'

He ignored that. 'Would a testimonial from me help?' She could add that to her portfolio and it would help provide the kudos she needed.

Her face lit up as she pulled his robe around her. 'Yes!'

'Consider it done.'

'Oh, Beau, thank you and—'

He waved her thanks away. 'Meet me in the kitchen in five.'

He cooked because, despite evidence to the contrary, he did know his way about a kitchen and he wanted to cook for her, wanted to care for her. Last night—and this morning—had been special. He wanted her to feel special too.

They dug into their food with gusto. Once the worst of their hunger had been sated, he eased back in his chair. 'Chloe, tell me, what's the worst thing that would happen if you couldn't pay the bank back?'

Her knife and fork clattered to her plate. 'I'd lose the home Mark and I made together.'

'Do you the love the house?'

'Of course I do! It's where we planned to have a family and *everything*.'

She might've felt that she'd said goodbye to Mark in some significant way, but clearly she wasn't ready to let him go completely. 'You want to keep living there although he's gone?'

Her eyebrows grew fierce. 'I don't see why not. It's not like I'm ever going to have another long-term relationship.'

Everything inside him stilled. 'Why not?'

She leaned towards him. 'Because losing someone you love is too hard. I feel as if I lost the last two years of my life, Beau. I'm not going through that again.'

But she had such a big heart. She deserved someone who'd love her and cherish her and look after her.

'Besides, the house is close to the garden centre, and once I've made enough money to get out of debt, I'll throw all of my energies into building up the design side of things there.'

His heart began to pound. 'Is that really the life you want? It seems to me that working in a garden centre would stifle your talents, rather than making the most of them.' And working with Mark's family would certainly stifle her love life. 'You think you'd be content designing suburban backyards instead of making over the gardens of grand estates or parks?' Which was clearly where her talents lay.

She opened her mouth but he pushed on. 'Think about it. You were forced to take drastic measures—like pitch for a high-status job like the one you landed here—but can you deny your enthusiasm for it? You can try telling yourself it's because circumstances demanded you needed to do something big to bring in a decent amount of money fast, but I've seen the way your whole being lights up when you're in the garden out there. Your vision is *big*. Would working at the garden centre bring you the same sense of satisfaction?'

She stared at him as if she didn't know what to say.

He pointed at her. 'You could sell up and strike out on your own. For heaven's sake, you should be designing amazing gardens—both public and private—not talking customers through the pros and cons of x mulch versus y mulch or how to deadhead azaleas.'

'Mark and I planned—'

'Mark isn't here any more.' He said the words as gently as he could. 'Why do you feel honour-bound to lead the life you planned together without him?'

'You want me to reimagine my whole life?'

'Why not? Your whole life was turned upside down after Mark's accident. Why not decide what *your* passion is and chase that instead?'

CHAPTER EIGHT

THE WORDS HELD a temptation Chloe didn't want to acknowledge. They made her feel as if she were betraying Mark in a more fundamental way than making love with Beau had.

Making love with Beau hadn't felt like a betrayal, but a step forward. This though…?

She leapt up to pace, flinging out her arms. 'You're a fine one to talk about chasing one's passion. Look at you, hiding away here like some tragic Victorian madam. It's laughable! And a damn shame too, if you ask me.'

'Nobody did ask you.'

His lips had turned white and he'd become as icy as she was heated. 'Oh, I see.' She slapped a hand to her head as if in sudden enlightenment 'I ought to follow my passion and the things that bring me joy, while you get to hide yourself away from all the things that remind you of your former life.'

He shot to his feet. 'I'm building a new life!'

'No, you're not! You're just trying to hide from your old one, trying to hide from all that you've lost and desperately want back. And the walled garden is a sticking plaster that isn't going to cut it, not in the long term.' He deserved better. Couldn't he see that? 'And what's the real reason you continue hiding out here? Because you're scared people are going to stare at your face and point. *Get over it!*'

'Easy for you say!'

'I'd rather be coming to terms with scars than coming to terms with my husband's death.'

Her words echoed in the sudden silence. Had it been unworthy of her to hurl them at him?

She dragged in a breath, tried to moderate her breathing. 'You love making documentaries. You came alive when you spoke to camera about the pipistrelles. It was amazing. And you want to know why it matters so much to me?' She ploughed on before he could tell her he couldn't care less. 'The world needs people like you, Beau. People who can show the rest of us the small changes we can make in our lives that will have a big impact on our forests and oceans, people who teach us to value all living things and can convince us to make the sacrifices necessary to ensure those living things get a chance to survive…people who make us care.'

He stared at her as if he had no idea what to say.

'You made us care about things that really matter, Beau.' Tears burned her eyes. 'It'll be a tragedy if you don't keep doing that.'

'I was dumped.' His hands clenched. 'My network dumped me.'

'So maybe you can't keep doing it in the same way. Maybe you need to find another way, even if it is on a smaller scale. Start your own YouTube channel and do all the filming yourself or hook up with a community channel or something. Or think bigger.'

One eyebrow rose.

'You have a lot of money, right?' She hitched up her chin. 'So buy a TV network of your own. Nobody could sack you then.'

He leaned towards her, brow furrowed. 'Damn it, Chloe, you have no idea how these things work and—'

'But you do!'

He stilled. Blinked. She didn't know if her words had struck a chord. Or hit a sore spot.

What she became increasingly sure of was that the heat that had engulfed her was now less about temper and more about desire. She couldn't stop her gaze from travelling over the powerful lines of his body, or stop remembering all the ways they'd given each other pleasure.

She wasn't sure if he recognised the new direction her thoughts had taken or not, but his shoulders lost their tension and while he still scowled at her, it had lost its heat. 'Clearly, just because we've become lovers, doesn't mean we've learned to be more polite to each other or less inclined to speak our minds.'

'I don't see why that should change. You think I'm being an idiot and weren't shy about telling me so. I don't see why I shouldn't tell you that you're being an idiot too.'

'I didn't call you an idiot!'

'It's what you meant.' She glared at him. 'It doesn't mean I don't still trust you. Or like you.'

'Ditto.' His nose curled, but she could've sworn there was a hint of a smile in his eyes.

He raked her up and down with that hot gaze and everything inside her clamoured for him and the release she knew he could bring her. 'I can't get enough of you at the moment,' she blurted out, unsure if that was a good thing or a bad thing. 'You are so *hot.*'

'And you are temptation personified.'

She glanced at the kitchen chair she'd pointed to last night and then raised an eyebrow. 'Yes?'

'Yes,' he growled back.

She pushed him into the chair and followed him down, straddling his lap, and he started laughing. Things inside her suddenly soared free and she found herself laughing too. And then her mouth met his in a hot hungry dance and blotted everything else from her mind.

Later that afternoon, lying naked on a thick rug in the baronial hall, a fire crackling in the hearth and the lights of the tree twinkling, and with Beau's broad chest beneath her cheek, Chloe couldn't remember feeling so replete or when she'd last felt such peace.

Obviously she must've done in the past with Mark. They'd been so in love. But peace had eluded her since his death, and she welcomed it now. Maybe that was why she allowed her mind to go over all that Beau had said over breakfast about finding a new direction for her life.

'Do you really think I could make a go of it if I went out on my own as a garden designer?'

The hand tracing intriguing patterns on her back stilled before beginning its idle tracing again. 'I do. You're wonderfully talented. You can look at a space and see what it can become. When I first saw the initial plans and the sketches you'd made for the walled garden, they blew me away.'

Really?

'You'd captured everything I said was non-negotiable, but you put them together in a way I hadn't envisaged, and then you added elements I hadn't considered. I found myself wanting those elements more than my original vision. It was both familiar and not. You made it better than I could imagine.'

She lifted her head. 'What a lovely thing to say.'

He glanced down at her. 'It's the truth.' And she could tell he meant it. 'That's why the contract went to you, even though you didn't have the same level of experience as some of the other bidders. You have a vision that's unique. It's a gift. And I think once the right people realise it, you're going to be in serious demand.'

She rested her cheek against his chest again, pulled the blanket up a few extra inches to keep him warm.

'Tell me about the garden centre. Why did you and Mark decide to go into business with his family?'

She nestled into him, relishing his warmth and vitality, along with his clean scent and the very *maleness* of him. He was right. Sex for fun could be a *very* enjoyable experience.

'I think I mentioned before that Mark was doing a Business degree when we met.'

'You did.'

'His parents owned a little local hardware store in the south-west of Sydney and the nursery next door came up for sale just as we were finishing up our degrees.' She shrugged. It'd felt like a no-brainer at the time. 'We took it as a sign that we should combine the two businesses. I could take care of the nursery side of things with a view to moving into garden design once we were in the black, Mark was to take care of the business side of things, while his mum and dad headed up the hardware side of the business.'

He shifted slightly and then pulled her even closer. If he did too much of that, there wouldn't be conversation again for a very long time. How could she still be so hungry for this man?

'But you'd won an award. You could've found a position with a big-name firm doing large-scale design work. Didn't you resent not being able to follow that path?'

'I won that award while I was still at uni, Beau—for one of my assignments. One of my tutors entered it without my knowledge. Don't get me wrong, I was over the moon to have won, but I hadn't figured out what career direction I wanted to take at that stage.' She'd been too in love. 'And the thought of Mark and I being able to work together, well…we both thought that was wonderful.'

'I see.'

She heard the frown in his voice and sat up, keeping the blanket clasped to her chest in the interests of modesty. Not that modesty had been all that important to her an hour ago. 'What?'

He eased into a sitting position and then picked her up and moved them to the sofa, the two of them propped up on opposite ends facing each other, their legs entangled. The blanket was big enough to cover them—from her chest to his waist. If she tugged it just a little, though, it'd slide down and—

'Behave,' he said with a low laugh, and she found herself grinning. 'Before we get side-tracked, I want you to know that my *I see* wasn't about you. It was about me.'

'How so?'

'I'm clearly a selfish sod, but I'm glad I didn't

meet anyone while I was studying, that I felt free to follow my own dreams.'

He'd started to massage her foot and it took all of her strength not to start purring. 'That's not being selfish. It's just being focussed. You always knew you wanted to make documentaries?'

'I always knew I wanted to be a natural historian, and the moment I took a documentary elective, the moment I started talking to a camera…' He shrugged. 'You're right, it felt as if something inside me had come alive.'

Did that mean he was considering what she'd said to him earlier? She bit the question back. She'd said more than enough on the subject for one day.

'I'm glad I had nothing distracting me from following the path I'd started to see for myself.'

She'd fallen in love with a person. He'd fallen in love with a career. But what if she hadn't fallen in love with Mark? What if they'd never met?

The thought made her blink. Maybe she'd have gone on and made a name for herself, just as Beau had said. Maybe she'd have been gloriously happy and successful.

The thought shook her to her foundations. She'd always thought fate had thrown her and Mark together, but maybe there wasn't just one path a person was meant to follow, one path that would make them happy. Maybe there were multiple paths that led to all different kinds of fulfilment and happiness.

So what if she lost the house? Maybe she could get a trendy apartment in the inner city. Maybe she could travel the world designing amazing gardens and working with designers she revered.

A strange new energy stirred inside her.

'Did you enjoy working at the garden centre?'

She pulled her mind back. 'In the early days it was exciting. It was great to have free rein to do what I wanted. And we developed a great team. The staff became like family. I was proud of what we were achieving.'

He nodded. 'Good.'

'Of course, that all changed when Mark died.'

He held her foot to his chest, just above his heart, and she could feel the strong beat through her sole. 'I'm sorry that happened, Chloe.'

'I know.' But would she have eventually become bored with the garden centre? Would she have wanted the bigger dreams Beau had held up to her? 'If I sold the house I'd be able to pay the bank back and help the garden centre get back in the black. I'd be able to repay Mark's family for carrying me as a deadweight for the last two years.'

'I bet deadweight isn't how they see you.'

'They wouldn't. They're lovely people. But it's the truth. They've been carrying me for far too long and that has to stop.'

'Good for you.'

'You might have a point, Beau. Maybe I do need to rethink my direction and start dreaming different dreams.'

His fingers stilled on her foot. 'You mean that?'

'I don't know.' It scared her senseless, but beneath it lay a thread of something that felt right too. At the very least it deserved consideration. 'But I'm prepared to make a deal with you.'

His eyes narrowed. 'What kind of deal?'

'That I'll think very carefully about all you said to me earlier, if you'll do the same about what I said to you.'

He tensed, and she sensed his immediate antipathy. Before he could reject it outright, she added, 'All I'm asking you to do is *think* about it. To not dismiss it out of hand until you've considered it from all angles. Maybe it's not the right way forward. But maybe it is. And if it is then you need to work out a way to make it happen.'

His nostrils flared and his hands tightened about her foot, but eventually he let out a breath and his grip eased. 'All I'm promising is to think about it? And in return you will too?'

She nodded. 'But this is a real promise, not just something either one of us is paying lip service to. If you make the promise, I'm trusting you to keep your word.'

His gaze darkened. 'If I make you any promise, Chloe, I *will* keep it.' He settled back against the arm of the sofa. 'If I agree, will you let me see your breasts?'

She choked back a laugh. 'Yes.'

'Then we have a deal.'

She immediately lowered the blanket, laughter bubbling up through her, and when his laughter joined hers it made her feel invincible.

Beau only made the promise because every instinct he had told him Chloe would be happier following a new direction—one she forged for herself. She shouldn't be shackling herself to an old dream that would prove empty and unsatisfying without Mark. She deserved something more than a life throbbing with loss.

Besides, he'd only promised to think about it. That was all. How hard could it be?

He rolled his shoulders. Considering how much he'd avoided thinking about it for the last fourteen months, he suspected it'd be awful. But...

Maybe it was necessary. Maybe it'd help him move into the future with a lighter heart.

'There's something else I want to ask of you.'

The tone of Chloe's voice had all the fine hairs on his arms lifting, though he kept his voice deliberately light. 'What's that?'

'You said you want to ease your grandmother's worry?'

The deeper reason for his grandmother's concern, the reason she'd enlisted Stephanie and

George's help to ensure he didn't descend into the extremes of despair that had led his father into addiction, all while doing her best not to stifle him, made him sick to the stomach. He should've realised it sooner. She deserved better from him.

'Beau, you study the natural world.'

She leaned towards him and the blanket shifted slightly, hinting at the shadows between her breasts, and his mouth went dry. For a moment all he could think about was making love with her again.

'You have Exmoor practically on your doorstep. You should be taking advantage of it and losing yourself there.'

Things inside him shied away in protest. At the same time, though, the natural historian in him raised its head. The temptation had been rattling around inside him ever since she'd mentioned Exmoor the other night.

But he would inevitably come across other ramblers, maybe even other researchers. And what if the press got wind of it and came hunting him again? He couldn't stand a repeat of that media circus.

She leaned forward even further. He did what he could to keep his gaze on her face rather than her chest. 'Before I go back to Australia, I want you to take me on an excursion to Exmoor and show me something amazing.'

What on earth would she consider amazing?

He scowled, but he suspected it lacked its normal heat because she merely eased back and raised an eyebrow, not looking the slightest bit intimidated. 'And what do I get in return?'

'You get to show your grandmother a piece of video footage that you take there and the satisfaction of knowing you're easing her mind.'

She made a strong argument. Knowing he was spending time in the national park would ease his grandmother's mind as nothing else could. It ought to have occurred to him sooner.

'And I'll cook you turkey with all the trimmings on Christmas Day,' she added, as if she could get around him via his stomach.

He stared at her. Her mother would love the photos of a Christmas dinner with all the trimmings. 'You'd do that for me, even though you're not all that interested in celebrating the season?'

'Absolutely.'

He held out his hand and they shook on it.

'I've thought of something else your families would love, Chloe.'

That bright gaze swung back.

'What if we were to video-call with them on Christmas morning, and show them how much we're enjoying all the trappings and outline our plans for the day—including that roast turkey dinner?'

She hesitated. 'Are you sure you wouldn't mind appearing on screen with me?'

Not if it meant easing her mother's mind. 'Like I said, I liked your mum. It'd be nice to see her again.' And he was curious about the rest of her family—her dad and brothers and sister. It'd be nice to put faces to names.

'You're an absolute sweetheart, you know that, Beau Diamond?'

If she kept looking at him like that he was going to have to kiss her.

'There is a catch, though.' He bit back a grin. 'It means buying each other Christmas presents.'

She blinked and a slow smile transformed her face, and it made his heart bump and bounce in his chest. 'You're talking about making up silly Christmas stockings for each other, aren't you?'

He nodded.

'*That* is inspired.'

He wished her mother could see her face now. Because it was clear to him that Chloe's Christmas spirit was beginning to return. The thought that he'd had a hand in that lifted him as nothing else had in the past fourteen months.

'Right.' He clapped his hands. 'Sounds like we'll be visiting the Christmas markets in the village tonight.'

While the markets weren't huge, they were a long-established tradition and Ballingsmallard was picture-postcard-pretty, which meant they did draw people from further afield. Beau was careful to keep his beanie drawn low down on his forehead and his scarf wrapped up high to shield his face.

'The presents need to be surprises.' Chloe pointed one mittened finger at him. 'That's part of the fun.'

He'd do anything to keep that smile on her face. 'Let's split up, then, and meet back here in an hour.'

He hadn't realised before that Christmas shopping could be so much fun. In the past he'd always considered it a bit of a chore, but trying to figure out what to put in Chloe's Christmas stocking— what would make her smile and laugh—had him glued to the task. While he was at it, he found a beautiful silk scarf he knew his grandmother would love. He'd send it express post to Florence, so she had it in time for Christmas.

He was back at the designated spot with plenty of time to spare, but he didn't mind waiting. It was a cold night, but he'd rugged up warm. A glance at the sky informed him they were in no danger of rain…or snow. The stars twinkled brightly and—

He stilled…and clapped a hand to his brow. Chloe had said she wanted to see *something amazing*. He knew exactly what he'd show her. And it'd blow her socks off.

A few minutes later she came running up, her breath misting the air and a smile on her lips. 'I love the Christmas markets!'

He pointed at all her bags. 'I bet the vendors

loved you too. Did you leave anything for anyone else to buy or did you clear the stalls out?'

'I had to buy gifts for everyone at home and… oh, it was just irresistible. I forgot how much fun it was to buy presents.'

'What did you get?'

He pretended to crane his neck to peek at her bags. Laughing, she hid them behind her back. 'Never you mind, Mr Stickybeak.'

'Dinner at the pub?'

'Sounds perfect.'

Much, much later, when she was wrapped up in his arm and he was drifting off to sleep, Beau couldn't help but think the entire day had been perfect.

All the fine hairs on his arms suddenly lifted and his eyes snapped open. He'd been here before, feeling on top of the world and thinking everything was perfect. It had been a *good* day, but this was all temporary. He'd been a fool to forget it.

Letting out a breath, he relaxed back against the pillows. He knew the score. He could enjoy this while it lasted without thinking it meant anything. It was simply all of those feel-good endorphins their lovemaking had released. He closed his eyes. He wasn't a fool. He had no intention of mistaking them for anything else.

'We're going out?'

'Rug up warm,' he ordered, tossing her one of

his warmest woollen jumpers. 'Put that on over your own jumper, wear two pairs of socks under your boots, plus you'll need your gloves *and* mittens, and your coat.'

Bending down, she glanced out of the window. 'But it's going to be dark soon.'

'Hence the reason you need to rug up warm.'

'We're going out *again*? But that'll be two nights in a row.' She stared at him, hands on hips. 'Careful, Beau, you're in danger of turning into a social butterfly.'

Her words made him throw his head back and laugh. In a little while she was going to retract that accusation roundly. She stared, her lips parting as if she'd found it suddenly hard to get air into her lungs. As if the sight of him laughing did something to her. Their gazes caught and clung. Maybe going out could wait till tomorrow night and—

With an effort he dragged his mind back to the task at hand. The weather was changing tomorrow, and he'd promised to show her something amazing. Besides, he was eager to see her reaction. He wanted to see if she'd love it as much as he did. 'C'mon, chop-chop. Time's a wasting.'

Without further ado, she did as he said.

She jumped in the Land Rover a short time later when he held the door open for her, but when they set off in the opposite direction to the village she began to pepper him with questions. 'It will all become apparent soon,' he promised, holding a finger to his lips.

She subsided with the faintest of frowns, and a short while later he pulled the car off the side of the road. 'We're here.'

'Where's here?'

'Exmoor.'

Her gaze sharpened.

'You said you wanted to see something amazing.'

'I do.'

'Then follow me.'

He shrugged on the backpack before adjusting her scarf so the cold air couldn't touch her neck and throat and then took her hand and started along a trail.

'How far are we walking?'

'A mile in and a mile out.'

'But that means it's going to be dark by the time we come back.'

'It's a popular trail, well maintained, and I brought a torch.'

'What are we going to see?'

She was practically jumping up and down with excitement and it made him grin. 'Do you trust me?'

She stilled, suddenly serious. 'With my life.'

Her words speared into him, making him feel about twenty feet high, and invincible. He had to clear his throat before he could speak. 'Then wait and see. Just enjoy the walk.'

With a nod, she did as he said. And as they walked side by side in the twilight a peace he had never known—not even prior to his accident—stole over him. He didn't know what it meant, but he sensed a part of himself that had been badly damaged was starting to heal, and probably not before time. Maybe it was a gift of the season, but mostly he suspected it was due to the woman beside him.

He'd try and work out what it all meant another day. For the moment, all he wanted to focus on was showing her something amazing.

When they reached their destination, he pulled a blanket from the pack and spread it on the ground and seated her on it, before laying a second blanket over her lap. Pouring them both mugs of hot chocolate, he had her hold them as he dropped three marshmallows in each.

She gave a delighted laugh. 'You came well prepared.'

'And the *pièce de résistance*…' With a flourish he pulled out fat slices of fruitcake.

'If my hands weren't full, I'd clap!'

He snapped a picture of her to send to her folks, before settling beside her and taking one of the mugs. They sat there, shoulders and knees brushing, sipping their steaming chocolate and munching cake as the darkness gathered around them.

'So,' she eventually whispered, 'what are we waiting for? Badgers?'

'They're not very active at this time of year.'

'Red deer?'

'We should be so lucky.'

Her brow creased as she turned to him. 'Owls?' Her face suddenly lit up. 'Bats?'

He could've hugged her for that. 'Look up, Chloe,' he said gently.

She did as he bid, blinked as if to clear her vision, and then the breath left her on a whoosh. 'Oh, Beau,' she breathed in a reverent whisper.

He nodded. It was almost impossible to describe. 'You said you wanted to see something amazing.'

'I'd have never dreamed this in a million years.'

'In 2011 Exmoor National Park was designated an International Dark Sky Reserve. It's one of the darkest places in England, and one of the best places to stargaze.'

She rose to her feet, her eyes not leaving the sky. 'I've never seen anything more spectacular in my entire life.'

The sky was an explosion of stars—black velvet dotted with sparkling diamonds—the Milky Way spreading in an arc above them so dense with individual stars it made the mind boggle. Staring at it made him aware of the vastness of the universe, made him aware of the smallness of his own troubles. He couldn't say why, but staring up at all of that beauty gave him hope.

She swung back. 'I know next to nothing about astronomy.'

He gestured her back to the blanket, pulled her down to sit between his legs, her back resting against his chest as he pulled the blanket around them both.

He pointed out Venus and Mars, traced out the constellations of Ursa Major and Cassiopeia for her, relishing her warmth and wonder.

She pointed. 'How far away is that star?'

Light years didn't mean much to the average person. 'If you were to jump in the fastest rocket humankind has ever built, it would take seventy thousand years to reach that star.'

'No way,' she breathed, nestling back against him. 'That's awesome.'

Chuckling, he pressed a kiss to her hair. They sat like that for a long time, just drinking in the wonder and the beauty, but he knew he'd have to rouse her soon. It was cold and he didn't want her getting a chill.

As if reading the direction of his thoughts, she turned in his arms and kissed him with a deep heartfelt gratitude that made his heart beat hard. 'Thank you, Beau. Thank you for bringing me to this wonderful place. I'll never forget it.'

'I was worried you'd think I was cheating bringing you here at night time.'

She shook her head. 'That—' she waved at the sky '—is amazing.'

He shrugged, trying not to get too caught up in her praise. It was such a small thing that he'd done. 'I can bring you back to Exmoor during the day if there's anything in particular you want to see too,' he surprised himself by adding.

'I want to see really old forest,' she confessed.

'Too easy.'

What on earth…?

Ignore it. Go with the flow.

She beamed at him, and it was the only reward he needed.

The following week passed in an energising routine of gardening and lovemaking, and long conversations beside a warm fire. In between times Chloe cooked up a storm, though she couldn't seem to master shortbread, while Beau continued his pipistrelle research.

His mobile phone pinged, but he finished reading the latest research paper he'd found online before glancing at it. It was probably just his grandmother letting him know she'd received the parcel he'd sent.

He turned the screen towards him and blinked. What on earth…? It was from his agent. He hadn't heard from Bryce in months.

He opened the message and everything inside him turned to ice. Following the enclosed link, he watched the footage of himself in his own garden talking about pipistrelles and it was all he could do not to throw his head back and howl.

Swinging to his computer, he checked all of the social media sites—Facebook, Twitter, TikTok—he was trending on all of them. And the full effect of his scars on the bigger screen had his hands clenching to fists.

There was only one person who could be responsible for this, and the sense of betrayal sent pain ripping through his chest. How could Chloe have done this?

He'd trusted her.

Seizing his phone, he started for the kitchen, the storm raging in his heart black, ugly and demanding an outlet.

CHAPTER NINE

AT THE SOUND of Beau bowling into the kitchen, Chloe turned with the oven trays in her hands. She'd been making spiced cookies and the kitchen smelled like cinnamon and spice and every good thing. 'Which ones look better? The snowmen or the stars?' She frowned. 'Or maybe I should've just stuck with circles.'

She glanced up and dropped the trays to the table, the cookies immediately forgotten. Beau looked as if the sky had fallen in! 'What is it?' Had something happened to his grandmother? She moved across to take his hand, but he pulled away.

'What were you thinking?'

She flinched at the fury in his voice—fury reflected in the flashing blue of his eyes and the tight set of his mouth. She took a step back, searching her mind for what she could have done to make him so mad.

He thrust his phone towards her. She took it, glancing at the screen and her jaw dropped. The video she'd taken of him in the garden was playing on the screen. Her heart pounded up into her throat. It already had over eight hundred thousand views on social media and it'd only been uploaded four hours ago.

'How did this...?'

He plucked the phone from her fingers, his face growing stony and grim. 'You're going to play the innocent and deny you've any knowledge of this?'

He thought *she'd* uploaded it?

She clenched her hands, waiting for her temper to fire to life, waiting for ugly words to claw at her throat, words she had no intention of holding back. She waited for it to overtake her so she could tell him what a paranoid piece of work he was and ask who did he think he was to accuse her of such a thing. But the anger remained inconveniently absent. In its place was an overwhelming urge to burst into tears—not just tears, but ugly, snotty, entire-body sobbing.

The kind of sobbing that you couldn't help because your heart had been broken.

What the hell? She clenched her hands harder. Her heart *wasn't* broken.

And yet that searing anger still didn't come to her rescue.

His lip curled. 'Nothing to say?'

She nodded at his phone. 'I had nothing to do with that.'

He bent down to glare into her face, his eyes flashing, and deep in their depths she recognised the betrayal he felt, but that did nothing to ease the screaming ache in her chest or the nausea churning in her gut.

'I don't believe you.'

She swallowed the lump in her throat, holding

his gaze. 'All of your proclamations of friendship, all your assurances that you trusted me, were lies? Why? To get me into bed with you?'

His head rocked back as if she'd slapped him. 'Don't try and put this onto me.' His lips thinned. 'Why did you do it?'

'I will repeat it again, I had nothing to do with that.'

'There *is* no one else. You, me and my grandmother are the only people who had that footage, and my grandmother would never do something like that to me.' He stared at her, his eyes throbbing. 'Is it because you really can't face the thought of losing the house you bought with Mark? And selling that piece of video means you won't have to?'

She shook her head. He was in deadly earnest and it took all her strength not to fall into the nearest chair and drop her head to her hands. 'I thought we were friends,' she choked out.

A spasm passed across his face. 'Or did you think you were helping me? Did you think this would somehow reinvigorate my career?' His brow pleated as if he was searching for a less ugly reason for her supposed betrayal. 'Damn it, Chloe, you don't have the right to force my hand like that! You—'

His phone rang. 'Grandmother,' he said, pressing it to his ear. 'Yes, I've seen it.' His face tightened. 'It's everywhere. I expect the whole world has seen it.' He listened and then he froze. '*You* uploaded the video.'

And so the mystery was solved.

He swung to face her, but she was already turning away. Very quietly she let herself out of the back door, winding a scarf around her throat as she went and shrugging into her coat.

Grabbing tools from the garden shed, she headed straight for the walled garden. She didn't even consider which from the array of tools to use. Shrugging off her coat and scarf, she grabbed the sledgehammer and immediately set to work dismantling the wall of the second of the garden beds that needed to be completely rebuilt. George had already demolished the first.

She pounded at it with the same savagery that Beau's accusation had pounded at her, the shocks reverberating up her arms and through her entire body. She kept it up until her whole body ached, until her mind and heart finally—*thankfully*—went numb.

So what? So what if Beau hadn't trusted her after all? So what if they weren't, in fact, friends? So what if it had all been a lie? The fact their budding friendship was destroyed was disappointing, but she'd get over it.

Inside her something shrivelled and withered, but she ignored it.

Halting to wipe sweat from her eyes, she half

turned to find Beau sitting on the low wall of the neighbouring garden bed.

He immediately stood. 'Chloe, I don't know what to say.'

'I believe sorry is the traditional approach.'

'I am sorry. More sorry than you can know.'

'I expect you are,' she agreed, abandoning the sledgehammer for a hoe, and setting to work at extracting a stubborn clump of agapanthus. She loved agapanthus, but they had no place in this particular garden bed. Her lips twisted in the briefest, and probably bitterest of smiles. Now there was an apt metaphor.

'Chloe, I'm sorry I jumped to conclusions. I saw that piece of video and...'

'And I was the obvious culprit.'

'When I saw the number of views I panicked.'

He'd turned grey, and a part of her did feel sorry for him, sympathised. Even understood.

'I suddenly saw my life turning back into the circus it was fourteen months ago and I—' He broke off, shaking his head, looking haggard... exhausted...haunted. 'You copped the brunt of that, which was spectacularly unfair.'

Yep.

'I know it's asking a lot, but can you find it in that rather lovely heart of yours to forgive me?'

She broke off to lean on her hoe and raise an eyebrow. 'Was that an attempt at flattery?'

He met her gaze. 'You do have a big heart. I should've taken better care of it.'

She had to grudgingly admit that he could do a halfway decent apology when the occasion demanded it.

'Why did your grandmother do it?'

He dragged a hand down his face and seemed to brace himself, before meeting her eyes again. 'She's of the same opinion as you—that I should be focussing on reinvigorating my career, not hiding from it. She decided to force my hand. She thinks it'll prove to me that I still have an audience.'

'Have you forgiven her?' She didn't mean to ask the question but it slipped out. He nodded, but it was a heavy movement that couldn't hide his confusion or his sense of betrayal. It took everything she had not to walk over and put her arms around him.

He straightened. 'It's after lunchtime. And I promised your mother I wouldn't let you work too hard.'

She glanced at her watch. She'd been pounding away out here for a lot longer than she'd realised. She and Beau might no longer be friends, but she was still his temporary housekeeper.

'Can we continue this conversation back at the house over a bite to eat?'

As far as she was concerned, the conversation was over, but with a curt nod, she collected up

the tools—at least the ones he didn't grab first—
and they stowed them away before returning to
the house.

She made thick ham and cheese sandwiches
while he brewed a large pot of tea.

Sitting across from him at the table, she focussed on eating at least half a sandwich, even
though it sat like a lump of lead in her stomach.
Given all the calories she'd just burned she ought
to have worked up an appetite.

He remained silent, sipped his tea but didn't
touch his sandwich. She opened her mouth to tell
him to eat, but shut it again. He shook himself
with a sudden start, and she concentrated on eating her sandwich again.

'Chloe, when I returned to Dawncarden after I
was released from hospital, I was in…hell.'

She could see that.

'Not only were my dreams dust, but the people who'd once supported me were nowhere to
be found. That's when I realised they hadn't supported me so much as supported my success.
When I was no longer a success, they wanted
nothing to do with me.'

Her stomach twisted.

'I'd released myself from hospital early as I
couldn't stand the media circus, and my doctor
only agreed on the proviso that I hire a nurse.'

She frowned. What was he trying to tell her?

'Unbeknown to me, she took photos and tried to sell them.'

What?

'Luckily I was alerted by a contact in the media and my lawyer was able to take action and prevent the photos from seeing the light of day.'

She closed her eyes. As if he hadn't had enough to deal with.

'You once accused me of being paranoid about my privacy. But it's incidents like those that have made it hard for me to trust anyone.' His shoulders sagged as if a weight had dropped onto them. 'It's not an excuse. I should never have accused you like I did. But I thought knowing some of what I've had to deal with might help explain why I reacted like I did.'

It did help. A little. But it didn't change either the significance or the outcome of what had happened. She and Beau were over.

His eyes burned into hers. 'Can you forgive me?'

She shrugged. 'Yes.'

His entire face lit up, but then his gaze raked her face and that light died. 'But it doesn't change the fact that I messed up or that I hurt you.'

'I thought we were friends.'

'We are friends! Once you cool off, you'll see that.'

'*No!* We're employer and employee.'

'Client and contractor,' he corrected, something

flashing in his eyes. 'I swear, Chloe, I can make amends. I'll do everything I can to make this up to you and prove that you can trust me.' He shot to his feet, hands clenched. 'I know I messed up but—'

'The sex isn't just fun any more, Beau.'

He opened his mouth, frowned. 'I'm not talking about sex. I'm talking about friendship.'

'I want to talk about sex.'

He sat. 'Okay.'

'We were all about the good time and having fun, yes?'

He nodded.

'You just said that when I cool down, I'll see that we're still friends, but the thing is there's nothing to cool down from. I didn't get angry in the first place.'

He frowned.

She gestured between them. 'You and I do anger and snarling at each other really well, but my reactions have changed…evolved…become something different.'

'Different how?'

'Instead of flying off the handle at you I was just…' She moistened parched lips. 'I was gutted you'd think I'd do that to you.'

He paled.

'Anger wasn't my main emotion, hurt was.' She spoke words that *really* frightened her. 'And that made me realise that I'm in danger of feeling more for you than I'd planned to. I'm certainly in danger of feeling more for you than I'm ready to feel for anyone. I never wanted anything permanent. And neither did you. So the sex thing was great while it lasted, but it stops now.'

He stared at her and something in the backs of his eyes made her squirm but she kept her chin high. 'It's not *just* fun any more. It's threatening to become something deeper. I don't *want* deeper. And neither do you.'

His eyes flashed. 'So if you can't have sex you're not interested in friendship either?'

'Don't you dare!' She shot to her feet. 'I'm not the one who broke faith.'

'No, but you're sure as hell grasping for a reason to retreat now. And it's easier to blame me than to acknowledge your own fear.'

'What do you know? *Nothing!* As today has proved.'

His lip curled. 'Looks like you found your snarl again.'

'And you have no idea how happy I am about that.'

'Yeah, you look over the moon.'

God, what were they—children?

Closing her eyes, she dragged in a breath. 'Let's get one thing straight. I came here to do a job. I'm going to do that job—you'll get your fabulous garden while I'll get the satisfaction of a job well done. And then I leave. End of story.'

'End of story,' he agreed, slamming out of the kitchen.

She glared after him. 'I'm glad we got that sorted out,' she yelled at the top of her voice, but she couldn't help feeling she'd just lost something infinitely precious.

Beau slammed the door to his study and it reverberated with a satisfying crash, echoing throughout the house. He hoped it reached the kitchen. He hoped Chloe heard it and—

Who was he kidding? He wasn't angry with Chloe. He was furious with himself!

He paced the room like some restless caged beast. How could he have messed up so badly? What had he been thinking?

He hadn't been thinking, that was the problem. He hadn't stopped to question the suspicion that had overtaken him. He'd simply gone in half cocked, all guns blazing. So damn sure that another person had let him down.

His phone pinged with an incoming message. Bryce. He shoved the phone back in his pocket.

She'd told him repeatedly that she wasn't responsible, but he hadn't even given her the respect of listening. He'd refused to let go of his self-righteous anger, he'd refused to let himself feel vulnerable because…

His hands clenched and unclenched. Because he'd felt so damn gutted that she could betray him.

He'd been so damn afraid that sense of betrayal would overwhelm him he'd fed his anger in an effort to protect himself.

Instead he'd hurt a woman he'd come to respect above all others, and had lost a friendship that meant more to him than he'd realised. Chloe had forced him out of himself. She'd made him laugh. She'd let him snipe at her guilt-free—and he had because he'd needed it and so had she. She'd reminded him there were people in the world who didn't care about his scars.

She'd made him consider the possibility that he still had a career ahead of him. It might look different from the one he'd had previously, but so what? She'd made him focus on the good rather than the bad—the good in himself, but more importantly the good in other people. He had to find a way to win her friendship back.

He had to.

He'd miss the sex. With an ache that was physical. But the thought of losing Chloe's friendship was a thousand times worse. To know that when she left here in a month's time he'd never see her again...

He couldn't let that happen. Slamming to a halt, he ordered himself to think. His phone rang again. Bryce.

He turned it off and planted himself in his seat and did an Internet search on how to win a friend back. He was desperate. And he'd try anything.

* * *

Apologise. Hear the other side. Give them space. Make an effort.

Strengthen the bond by making them feel important by sharing things with them.

He'd written each of those items down, and he tried over the course of the following three days. He'd apologised again, but she'd told him there was no need, he'd already apologised and she knew he was sorry.

He was careful to keep his temper and impatience in check at the distance she deliberately created between them, at her aloofness. She clearly needed space. He'd give it to her if it killed him.

He invited her to play darts again on Thursday night. She declined. She didn't offer an excuse, and he didn't press her for one. He didn't fly off the handle. He kept his temper.

Actually, he didn't feel like yelling or losing his temper. He just ached that he couldn't bridge the gap. He ached at how much he'd hurt her. Chloe was the last person on earth who deserved to be hurt. She'd been through enough. She'd trusted him and he'd let her down.

He counselled patience. One article he'd read had said persistence was key. If there was one thing he could be, it was persistent. But he didn't want to be annoying.

So he went out alone, hoping his absence from Dawncarden would help her relax and feel not hounded or pressured by him. When he returned, empty-handed as he'd won nothing, he was careful to pass along the messages the other players had sent her. Those at least made her laugh.

He worked alongside her in the garden. They didn't chat as they previously had, but the physical exercise was good for the soul. And there at least they fell into a rhythm that was comfortable. That was when he felt most at ease. That was when his heart stopped burning for a few short hours.

He nearly swallowed his tongue when she glanced up from pressing rich brown earth around the roots of a freshly planted azalea and fixed him with a frown. 'I take it the constant pinging from your phone is your agent, Bryce?'

Bryce had called the house the previous day. Chloe had passed on the message, but he'd ignored it. He didn't have time for Bryce. He needed all of his focus to mend things with Chloe.

He pulled out his phone and glanced at it. 'Yep.'

'And I bet he's sent you multiple emails too.'

What did that have to do with anything? 'Probably. I haven't been checking my emails.'

'Why not?'

He shrugged.

'Have you checked your social media accounts?'

'God no.' He hadn't wanted to see the commiserations, the pity…the voyeuristic hunger of his so-called fans.

She thrust her trowel into the earth and rose. 'You promised you'd think about the possibility of returning to documentary-making in some way, shape or form. Was that a hollow promise?'

'No!'

But she was right. Since he'd screwed up so spectacularly, he hadn't given it any thought whatsoever. *Make an effort. Strengthen the bond by making her feel important by sharing things with her.*

He swallowed. 'I guess I've been avoiding thinking about it.'

She folded her arms when his phone pinged again. 'Surely step one in that process would be to talk to your agent about your options.'

His nose curled, even though he tried to stop it.

'What are you afraid of?'

She looked genuinely flummoxed. He didn't want to talk about it, didn't want to give voice to those fears. *Make an effort. Strengthen the bond by making her feel important by sharing things with her.*

He kicked at a weed. 'What if I don't like the options Bryce offers? Or, worse still, what if there aren't any options?'

Those treacle-dark eyes softened. A man could lose himself in eyes like those. She glanced away. 'He wouldn't be so persistent if you had no options.'

He stared and then squared his shoulders. If it

made her feel important, talking to Bryce would be a small price to pay. 'If I don't like what he has to say or I'm not interested in whatever he has to offer...'

She glanced back. 'Then you can politely decline and carry on as usual.'

He moistened dry lips. 'You want to come and read my email with me?'

Her eyes widened, but then she took a step away. 'It has nothing to do with me.'

'It has everything to do with you. If you hadn't extracted that promise from me, I'd—'

He dragged a hand down his face. *Be honest.* 'I wouldn't be opening myself up to this kind of disappointment.'

Her jaw dropped as if she hadn't even considered disappointment a possibility, and a part of him loved her for it—loved that she had so much faith in him.

He pressed his momentary advantage. 'I might need a friend nearby, as I read them.'

Her eyes flew to his.

'And in the absence of Stephanie, you'll have to do.'

He smiled and she rolled her eyes, but he suspected she was biting back a smile too.

'I'll make a deal with you. You come and eat spiced cookies and drink tea with me, while I check my emails, and I'll take you to see really old forest in Exmoor before you leave.'

'Deal!' She blinked as if startled at how quickly the word had left her.

He didn't give her time to rethink it, but collected up their tools. 'Okay, let's go do this.'

An hour later they stared at each other across the expanse of his desk.

She leaned towards him. 'Let me get this straight. Bryce is saying the TV network is offering you a contract to create, shoot and present your own nature series?'

He nodded, still trying to take it in. 'It's a rival network to the one I was with before.'

'And yet the old network is interested in reopening negotiations with you too.'

'In their dreams.' He wasn't going back to a network that had treated him so shabbily.

That didn't change the fact that another bona fide, legitimate network wanted him. *Him.* He grinned at her. He couldn't help it. She blinked before pointing at his computer. 'Why haven't you rung Bryce already, telling him that you want that deal?'

Because winning back her friendship was more important than anything else at the moment. He didn't just want to be the best documentary presenter the country had. He wanted to be a good person. And making things right with Chloe felt like the first step in reclaiming his humanity.

'Are you worried about people seeing your face and your scars?'

He rubbed a hand over his face. 'A little. The thought of being at the centre of another media circus doesn't fill me with a shred of enthusiasm.'

'You'll only be the centre of attention for a little while though. Until people get used to seeing you again.'

That was true. 'Maybe I can speed up that process by taking your advice and posting to my social media accounts again.'

Her face lit up. 'Exactly!'

'God, Chloe, you're making me think this could all be possible.'

She reached across and clasped his hand. 'It *is* possible, Beau. Ring Bryce.'

He did. Ending the call ten minutes later, he stared at her. 'Apparently I'm spending the next three nights in London.'

She clapped and did a happy dance. 'And when you get back you can show me those really old trees in Exmoor.'

'It's a deal.'

He hadn't left yet and already he wanted to be back.

The discussions he and Bryce had with the network went even better than Beau could have hoped. That piece of video that had gone viral on social media had revealed that there was an audience out there hungry for all Beau had to offer.

As a result, the network weren't only offering him a lucrative contract, but more importantly they were promising him full control over the direction the series would take. The thought that he would once again be filming and sharing his passion with a hungry audience should've filled his soul with fire.

He signed the contract on the second day of negotiations. The network treated him and his new team to the finest French champagne and a ridiculously expensive dinner in the private dining room of one of London's poshest hotels. His new co-workers were good-natured and full of enthusiasm. And yet, when he returned to his hotel room, something still felt as if it was missing.

What was wrong with him? He now had everything he'd said he ever wanted.

Chloe isn't here to share it.

And none of this would've been possible without her.

He rang, even though it was late. She answered on the second ring. Did he dare hope she'd been waiting to hear from him or was that wishful thinking? Shaking the thought off, he told her about the contract, about the team…about the ridiculously over-the-top menu at dinner.

She congratulated him, he knew she was happy for him, and he even felt that he'd made some ground in winning back her friendship. But as they rang off, he found himself prowling restlessly around his room.

And just like that, it all fell into place—like a key turning in a lock and revealing the secret behind the door. He should've realised it sooner. Much, *much* sooner.

He'd fallen in love with Chloe.

I'm never falling in love again. The words she'd spoken to him weeks ago rang in his mind now and he swore.

Squaring his shoulders, he thrust out his jaw. He wasn't letting the woman he loved walk out of his life without a fight. He'd prove to Chloe that he could make her happy. He'd do everything he could to make it as hard as possible for her to leave.

CHAPTER TEN

CHLOE MOOCHED AROUND the kitchen, not sure what was wrong with her. She'd tried making another batch of shortbread, but something had gone wrong with it. It had been so crumbly the only way to eat it had been with a spoon straight from the baking tray.

She made a fresh batch of spiced cookies instead. Beau gobbled those up as if they were going out of style. Except he wasn't here to gobble up anything. And now she had over three dozen of the darn things just sitting there, and *she* didn't want them.

She made a mental note to give a dozen to George.

She'd spent a long morning in the garden, making excellent progress until torrential rain had driven her indoors. She'd put a luscious beef and vegetable casserole into a slow oven and the kitchen was starting to smell delicious. She'd had a full day.

She shouldn't feel so restless.

Opening the refrigerator door, she glared at the bottle of champagne she'd made a special trip into the village for. Clearly they'd need to celebrate Beau's new contract when he got back tonight.

Because, hello…*good news*. So why wasn't she jumping up and down and excited?

She dropped down to the table, chin in hands. She *was* happy for him. This new contract was his dream come true. He deserved it. It was what she'd wished for him.

But that didn't stop her feeling flat. When she'd been working in the garden this morning she couldn't help wondering if he'd now spend any time there at all. She was working so hard to create the garden of his dreams, but…

But what? She'd still be paid for it and that was all that mattered.

She made tea. When she turned with teapot in hand she found Beau standing in the doorway. She blinked, but he didn't disappear. She gripped the handle of the teapot so hard her fingers started to ache, fighting an insane impulse to throw herself into his arms. 'I didn't hear you come in. You're early. Tea?'

'Yes, please.' His gaze raked her face and his eyes narrowed. 'You haven't been working yourself into the ground, have you, and doing stupid things like twelve-hour shifts in the garden?'

She bustled about getting him a mug and pouring the tea. 'Of course not. Even if I wanted to the weather made sure I couldn't.'

He grimaced. 'It was a bit wild and woolly on the roads, but I'd had enough of London and just wanted to get home.'

His words made something inside her lighten. She motioned him to a chair. 'Cookie?'

He grabbed several, and that strange restlessness dissolved. They settled back sipping tea and munching cookies. The house no longer felt strange and hollow. It felt exactly as it ought to.

The garden started to take shape and Chloe could see exactly what it would look like in a few years' time once it became established. She wondered if Beau would let her visit then.

Ha! He'd have forgotten who she was in another couple of years. She abandoned her trowel to press fingers into the small of her back. Besides, he'd be too busy shooting his marvellous documentaries in far-flung corners of the world and probably wouldn't have the time to appreciate the garden or—

'You're looking glum.'

She glanced up to find Beau watching her. He was supposed to be in his study, working.

She smoothed out her face. 'It's starting to look fabulous out here.' The garden beds had all been mended, and she'd started on the pruning, trimming and weeding. They'd even started some new planting.

'And that's a reason for looking glum?'

'Of course not.' For no reason at all, her heart started thump-thumping. 'Beau, I'm glad that you won't be burying yourself here in the garden. It's wonderful that you have a new contract.'

She gritted her teeth. It was. It really, *really* was.

'But?'

Those clear blue eyes focussed fully on her and things inside her pulled tight. Perspiration prickled her nape and the valley between her breasts, an ache started up low in her abdomen. How could she still want him so much? How could she remember so clearly the way he'd trail his fingers down her naked body and—?

She dragged her gaze away. Now that they were back on a *friendly* footing, she had no intention of threatening that by reinstating their friends-with-benefits arrangement. But the temptation hovered on the edges of her consciousness and it was an effort to remember all of the reasons why it would be a bad idea.

Besides, he clearly wasn't having the same difficulty. Her hands clenched. She had no right to resent that when *she'd* been the one to call a halt to things.

Gritting her teeth, she dug fingernails into her palms. She'd do the job she came here to do, get a sterling testimonial from Beau, before returning home and throwing herself into building up the design side of things at the garden centre.

Or you could sell the house, settle your debts, and begin a new life.

'Chloe?'

She shook herself. 'I was going to suggest you consider employing a gardener so the garden doesn't get so wild again.' Her voice came out husky and low. As if she was propositioning him.

He frowned.

Oh, Lord. Could he tell how much she still wanted him? She rushed into speech. 'Did you come looking for me for a reason? Is there something you needed?'

He straightened. 'There's something I wanted you to see.'

'Oh, but...' She gestured to the garden bed. She hadn't finished weeding this one yet.

He tapped a finger to his watch. 'You've been out here for four hours.'

She stared. 'Oh, my God! Lunch—'

'Can wait. I've been working on something all morning and I want you to see it. Besides, it's Christmas Eve and you deserve a holiday.'

He'd collected up her tools as he spoke, leaving her no choice but to trail after him. She stared at his back, her nose wrinkling. Did he want to show her the premise for some wonderful episode of his new series? Her shoulders drooped with every step she took. She wondered where it'd be filmed—the Amazon... Africa... Antarctica?

She shook herself. What on earth was wrong with her?

You will be enthusiastic.

You bet your sweet patootie she would be. She'd hounded the poor man until he'd realised his options weren't as limited as he'd feared. She'd challenged him to be brave and the least she could do now was be supportive.

'Are you sure you don't want me to make you a sandwich or—?'

He grabbed her hand and towed her through the house. 'I'll make ham and cheese toasties once we're done with this.'

'But I'm supposed to be housekeeper and—'

'My house. My rules.'

With a shake of her head, she submitted. Besides, ham and cheese toasties sounded delicious.

He planted her in his seat at the vast desk in his study. He clicked a button on the keyboard, a video appeared on the screen—a video of Beau in the garden. She leaned forward. This was part of the video diary she'd urged him to keep. And then the voice-over started.

There were three short videos in total, and she watched each of them transfixed.

When they were finished, she turned to him, opened her mouth but couldn't force a single word out.

He gestured at the screen. 'You wanted before and after shots of the garden for your portfolio, but I think these are a hundred times better. What do you think?'

He'd outlined in detail the plans she'd drawn

up, had revealed what each section of the garden would become, and he'd actually referred to her by name. He'd referred to her as a talented designer, had praised her to the skies, and said how lucky he'd been to find someone with her vision.

'The garden is your haven,' she blurted out. 'This—' she gestured wildly at the computer '—it's too much, Beau.' He might now have his brand-new documentary series to make, but she also knew how much his privacy still mattered to him.

'It's nowhere near enough,' he answered.

For a moment she imagined heat in his eyes, but then he blinked and it disappeared. 'You owe me nothing,' she whispered. He was still trying to make amends for losing her trust and it made her want to weep. 'You don't need to do this.'

'I know I don't need to, but I want to. You made me realise something, Chloe. In sharing my wonderful garden—the garden of my heart that *you're* creating—I won't be losing anything.' His hand closed over hers, squeezing it, before releasing it once again. 'It's still my garden. I can retreat here whenever I want, lose myself in its beauty and peace, and the abundance of life it holds. But in sharing it, I might inspire someone else to do something similar with their garden.'

'I...'

'You made me realise I needed to share my passion, not keep it locked up behind big stone walls.'

Her eyes stung and her throat thickened.

'I'll do more videos as work progresses, and I might even do an annual update. I'll send all of the video files to you to use in any way you see fit. I also plan to upload them to my social media channels.'

She could hardly get her head around the enormity of it all. 'That's the kind of promotion that makes careers, Beau.' Once his fans heard about her, she'd be inundated with offers of work.

'It only seems fair. You made me realise I still have a lot to offer the world. I want you to realise that you have a valuable gift of your own to share.'

If she dared.

'Hungry? C'mon, I'm starved.'

He was at the door before she could speak. 'Beau?'

He halted and turned.

Walking across to him, she stood on tiptoe and kissed his cheek. 'Thank you.'

CHAPTER ELEVEN

CHLOE LEAPT OUT of bed on Christmas morning and rushed to the window. Last night Beau had told her that there was every chance there'd be snow today. She didn't know why it felt so important that she get her white Christmas, only that something inside her hungered for it.

The moment she reached the window, a ray of sunshine emerged from the wall of cloud to sparkle on the dew, the grass and trees, but it didn't sparkle on snow. There wasn't a trace of that to be seen.

Her shoulders slumped.

In the next moment, she shook herself upright. It was Christmas morning and she was going to talk to her family in a little while and she had a lot to be grateful for. Yesterday, with Beau's gift of those videos, it had consolidated a bond of friendship she could no longer deny. After breakfast they'd exchange their silly Christmas gifts—she couldn't wait to see his face when he opened his—and her family would be delighted.

She hugged herself. The day was going to be perfect. Yesterday she'd been forced to acknowledge Beau's big-heartedness. It had made things right between them again and she was more grateful for that than she could say. She now knew that, no matter how much time passed, they would always be friends. With an excited wriggle, she rushed to get ready.

She and Beau met on the landing and they grinned stupidly at each other, before wishing each other a merry Christmas. He leaned down to kiss her, but somehow, rather than touching his lips to her cheek, their lips met. Had she turned her head to meet his lips? Or had he deliberately kissed her?

It was warm. It was brief.

It was irritatingly chaste.

He eased back to stare into her eyes, but then blinked and smiled, and she kicked herself for trying to read anything at all into it. 'Bacon and eggs?' she said with determined cheerfulness.

'Yes, please. I'll set the laptop up in the hall with the tree, and I mean to get a good blaze going.'

The house wasn't cold, the central heating saw to that, but the fire looked amazing when lit.

An hour later they were exchanging greetings with her family with the fire crackling in the background and that marvellous tree behind them. The time difference meant it was evening in Sydney, and her family sat around the dining table, which was set with leftovers. She had a sudden and piercing homesickness. 'Oh, I miss you all so much,' she blurted out.

'We miss you too, Chloe, honey! But you're

looking rosy-cheeked and well. Did you wake up to snow like you hoped?'

'No, despite Beau assuring me that there'd be snow today. But there's a big frost and it looks so pretty out.'

'Hey.' He feigned offence. 'The day has only just begun. There's plenty of time for snow yet.'

'She has her sights set on the sled stowed in the barn, Beau,' her mother said with a smile. 'Merry Christmas, pet, it's nice to see you again.'

'Merry Christmas, Mrs Jennings. And I haven't given up on the chance of sledding yet either.'

His grin pierced Chloe's heart. He looked so happy to chat to her mum again and meet the rest of her family, and the effort he was going to for her warmed her all the way through.

'Is that a stocking I see beneath the tree?' her father piped in.

Beau waggled his eyebrows. 'It appears that we both have Santa sacks under the tree.'

A chorus of 'Open them!' sounded from her family and with laughs they exchanged sacks. Like her, he'd wrapped the presents, and they couldn't help laughing as they tore off the wrapping.

He'd given her a bright red Christmas jumper with a reindeer on the front that she promptly put on, a new trowel, and a recipe book for shortbread that made her laugh—and everyone else when she told them about her so far disastrous attempts at baking shortbread. Her final present was a set of darts that had her grinning madly.

She'd bought him a pair of pyjamas splashed in a Christmas print of bright red and white candy canes. He stared at her, one eyebrow raised. 'It's a tradition in our family,' she told him. 'We all get Christmas-themed PJs.' Her family held theirs up for him to see and he grinned with so much delight her heart started to ache.

Next came a book on the art of insults, which had him laughing, and last of all he unwrapped the dartboard. With a grin, he held it up for her family to see. 'Guess what we'll be doing this afternoon?'

It was all simply *perfect*.

Beau glanced at Chloe after they ended the call with her family. She stared into the fire, rubbing a hand across her chest. He reached out and gripped her hand, imagining how much she must miss them.

'Okay?'

Her fingers tightened about his. 'Yes. Sorry! I just…we did it.' She drummed her heels on the floor as if she couldn't contain her delight. She reached across to grip his other hand. 'We did it! They're not worried or fretting or anxious about me. I didn't spoil their Christmas and…oh, I can't tell you how happy I am.'

She didn't have to. Her delight was evident.

'You didn't ruin their Christmas, Chloe. Not one jot. I mean, they clearly miss you, but they enjoyed our present opening every bit as much as we did.'

She eased away, a slight frown creasing her brow as if it hadn't occurred to her that she'd had fun too, as if her own happiness hadn't been part of the equation.

Oh, Chloe, sweetheart.

'Anyone who loved you, Chloe, would be happy and relieved to see you having fun and embracing the spirit of the season.' Including Mark, though he didn't say that out loud.

If Mark had truly loved Chloe, and he suspected he had, then he wouldn't want Chloe to close herself off from all the good things life had to offer. He didn't say that out loud either. Chloe already knew it. It was no longer Mark's memory that held her back but her own fear.

'I've never had a Christmas morning that was so much fun.'

That immediately pulled her out of her reverie. 'Truly?'

He shrugged. 'Maybe when I was very small, but the memories are hazy like they belong to someone else. Usually my grandmother and I spend Christmas together and it's a quiet affair. I mean, we exchange gifts and it's nice. I'm not complaining. It's just—' he gestured at the laptop '—that was a revelation.'

'And fun,' she said, nodding.

He made himself grin and ooze Christmas spirit. 'I can't help feeling it's the right way to do it. And I've no intention of stopping now.' He seized the dartboard. 'You ready for a Christmas darts tournament?'

'You bet.' But then her phone pinged with an incoming text. She read it and grinned.

His hands clenched. *Who* had made her grin like that?

She stowed her phone and glanced up, eyes bright. 'I did get you one more present.'

She had? His heart started to thump. Had that smile been for *him*?

He did what he could to school his face. *Be cool, Diamond. Don't jump to conclusions.* But in that moment it occurred to him that Chloe had feelings for him. Deeper feelings than either of them realised and it gave him hope. 'I got you something else too.'

She blinked. 'But…you shouldn't have!'

He shrugged. 'Pot? Kettle? Which one do you want to be?'

Which made her laugh. 'Well, let me get your present first.' She pointed. 'Stay right where you are and don't move. Promise?'

He crossed his heart. She disappeared in the direction of the kitchen. Had she baked him something amazing? Or maybe she'd bought him some wonderful plant for his garden? Or the house! If she had, he'd treasure it forever and—

'Close your eyes and hold out your hands,' she called out.

He did as she bid.

'Now keep them closed.' He could smell her as she drew closer, the scent of lavender merging with the scent of pine. He pulled it into his lungs, glorying in it. 'Careful now,' she murmured as she placed something soft in his hands, her hands curling around his and moving his arms so he cradled whatever it was against his chest.

Something soft that...wriggled.

'Open your eyes,' she whispered.

He glanced down to find he was holding a sleepy puppy that was starting to wake. Puppy eyes met Beau's as Beau lifted him until they were face to face, and the puppy promptly licked his nose before yawning.

Beau fell in love on the spot.

'He's a beagle cross, and is going to be a whole truckload of mischief. I organised him before you signed your new contract, but I did speak to Stephanie first, and she's more than happy to be a surrogate puppy parent when you're not here.'

Chloe hadn't wanted him all alone in this vast house. He couldn't speak for the lump that lodged in his throat.

'He's from a litter of puppies from one of the

local farms,' she babbled, 'and they were desperately looking for homes and—'

He reached out and pressed a finger to her lips. 'I love him. He's perfect.'

Her lips were perfect too, especially when they curved in a smile. He wanted to lean across and press his lips to hers and—

She shot back as if she read that thought in his face. His heart thumped and protested, but he did what he could to keep the smile on his face.

Rome wasn't built in a day.

'How on earth did you manage to hide him from me?'

'George collected him for me from the farm this morning, on his way to his daughter's for the day.'

He stroked a finger across the puppy's head. 'He's the most perfect gift I've ever received. You couldn't have given me anything I'd have loved more.'

Except your heart.

The words whispered through him and he glanced at the twinkling lights on the tree. Christmas was supposed to be a time of miracles, wasn't it? Maybe he'd get his very own Christmas miracle this year.

'His basket and food bowl and all the things he needs are in the kitchen. What are you going to call him?'

'Rudolph,' he decided, and she clapped her

hands, pronouncing it perfect for the little puppy. 'Rudy for short.'

Rudy had clearly had a busy morning because he yawned and curled up on Beau's knee and promptly fell asleep. Only then did Beau reach into his pocket and pull out the present he had for her. 'I saw this when I was in London and it made me think of you.'

She glanced at him uncertainly, but took it. 'You didn't have to get me anything else.'

'You didn't have to get me a puppy either, but that doesn't mean I'm not glad you did.'

She turned the present over in her hands. 'It won't bite,' he promised.

That made her smile and without any further ado she tore away the paper and then sent him a startled glance when she discovered the velvet box beneath. But when she opened the lid her lips parted on a silent exhalation. 'Oh, Beau, it's beautiful.'

She pulled the necklace from the box, and the diamonds glittered in the light.

'Please tell me these are crystals or cubic zirconia.'

'They're crystals or cubic zirconia,' he promptly replied. 'Actually, it doesn't matter what they are. What matters is, do you like it?'

'Yes.' The single word was fervent.

She'd taken her jumper off when she'd returned with the puppy and she swept her hair to the side, to catch the latch behind her neck, before straightening, her fingers dancing across it lightly. 'How does it look?'

From a thin bar of platinum, five white gold flowers rose—all different heights and shapes, their petals sparkling with diamonds. She'd probably have a pink fit if he told her how much it had cost. 'Perfect.'

She raced across the room to a low-hanging mirror and surveyed her reflection. 'Oh, Beau, it's the most beautiful thing I've ever seen.'

'The garden you're creating for me is more beautiful.' And she was more beautiful than all of the gardens of the world. 'But it suits you. I thought it'd be a memento of your time here.'

She turned. 'Thank you, Beau. I love it. It's perfect. But I don't need a memento of my time here. I'm never going to forget it.'

Her brow suddenly wrinkled as if the fact she'd never forget Dawncarden—and him? he crossed his fingers—perturbed her. He wasn't letting anything bother her today. 'Right, let's find Rudy's basket, and then you and I are having a darts tournament to end all darts tournaments. The winner gets to eat all the spiced cookies they want.'

They ate their huge dinner in the grand dining room at two p.m. because that was the tradition at Dawncarden, and they stuffed themselves so silly they could barely move. The roast turkey and baked potatoes, the Brussels sprouts and gravy, not to mention the plum pudding with brandy custard, were utter perfection.

Chloe glanced around and couldn't help but be secretly delighted by the sumptuousness of it all. 'There're enough leftovers to last a week,' she groaned.

Beau rubbed a hand across his stomach. 'That's one of the best things about Christmas. Besides, doorstop-sized turkey sandwiches are the best.'

Which sounded perfect for lunch tomorrow.

They played with Rudy, who was full of puppy playfulness and fun, but he fell asleep with the same kind of prompt solidness of a toddler. The way Beau looked at him—as if he were a miracle—made everything inside her ache and burn and want to hug him.

Oh, who was she trying to kid? She wanted to tear the clothes from his body and ravish him. Over and over. The burning attraction should've eased by now, but it hadn't. It had grown into a roiling, bubbling roar of blistering need. And try as she might, she couldn't seem to move beyond it.

'Look out the window, Chloe.'

Glad for the distraction, she leapt up and moved to the front window. She swung back, clapping her hands. 'Snow!'

'Told you.'

'Oh, my God!' She raced for the front door and launched herself outside.

Glancing upwards, she held her arms out and turned on the spot. Huge white flakes drifted down from the sky and settled over everything, utterly transforming the lawn, the trees, the fences. *Oh, this was glorious.* Opening her mouth, she caught a cold flake on her tongue. Spinning on the spot again, she found Beau watching her from the doorway, the hugest grin on his face.

Six weeks ago the man hadn't known how to smile, let alone grin.

'Merry Christmas, Chloe.' He ambled towards her with a lean-hipped grace that made her mouth go dry. He gestured heavenward, but his eyes didn't leave her face. 'You got your Christmas wish.'

She had. 'I—' She swallowed, but she couldn't look away. 'I so wanted a white Christmas. I can't believe it's happened.' But all she could see was him.

'Oh, ye of little faith.'

But his breath quickened and hers did too.

His gaze darkened. 'You look like an angel standing in the snow.'

The naked desire in his eyes stole her breath. She didn't know who moved first, her or him, but she found herself wrapped in his arms, and his mouth moving over hers with a reverence that had tears prickling her eyes.

He eased away, his throat bobbing as he swallowed. 'Sorry, I probably shouldn't have done that.'

'I wanted you to.' Her pulse jumped and jerked and her lips tingled. 'If we're being honest, I want to do a whole lot more than just kiss, Beau.' She tried to steady her breathing. 'I know I called a halt to that side of things, but maybe I was hasty and—'

'I want more.'

His eyes burned into hers, but his words pulled her to a halt. She frowned. 'But wasn't that what I was just saying...offering?'

He dragged a hand down his face and then braced his hands on his knees before straightening. 'You're offering me your body, Chloe, and while I'm burning for that too, I want more.'

Her breath hissed from her lungs as his meaning became clear. She took a step back.

'I want your heart, Chloe.'

CHAPTER TWELVE

No.

'I didn't mean to fall in love with you.'

Chloe wanted to block her ears against Beau's words. *No!*

'But I have. I know the thought of love scares you and so does the thought of turning your face to the future, but I love you. There's nothing I can do about it. But for what it's worth, I think love is worth risking everything for.'

He was wrong. So, *so* wrong. Losing love made you lose your very soul. It made you hurt so badly in ways you didn't know you could hurt. Losing love was brutal and pitiless and barbaric in its totality. 'No.' She took another step away from him, shaking her head. 'It's *not* worth it.'

He paled.

Her heart pounded so hard she thought it would leave bruises. 'I'm sorry, Beau. I didn't want you to fall in love with me. I thought I'd made that clear.'

He didn't answer.

She forced the words from an aching throat. 'My heart isn't on offer. I can offer you friendship and sex. But not love.' Never that.

The lines around his mouth deepened and his eyes dulled. She wanted to drop to her knees and sob. He kept his chin high, though. 'I think you need to look inside your heart, Chloe. I think the feelings you have for me are stronger than you want to admit. It's why, when I let you down, it hurt you so badly. It's why you tried to protect yourself so fiercely afterwards.' His gaze held hers. 'It's why you forgave me.'

'You're wrong,' she snapped, suddenly incensed. 'I forgave you because you're human and we all make mistakes and...' she waved her arms wildly about '...because we're friends and that's what friends do.'

'I think it's why you gave me a puppy. You didn't want me to be alone.'

'That's just... I mean... *You like animals!*'

'Chloe—'

'I'm not listening to any of this. It's nonsense!' She waved her hands in front of her face. 'I need some air. I'm going for a walk.'

His hand closed about hers, pulling her to a halt. She tried to tug free.

'Chloe!'

His voice, its volume, pulled her from her fog.

'I won't stop you going for a walk, but you need to put on a jumper, a scarf, your coat and boots.'

He was right. Without another word, she marched straight into the house and did exactly that.

'I know you don't want my company, but I ought to follow behind at a distance—'

'Don't you dare!'

'I won't as long as you make me a promise.'

She hitched up her chin and glared at him.

'There's not going to be enough snow for sledding until tomorrow, so it's safe enough for you to go walking now, but snow changes the landscape and can make it hard to get your bearings. Promise me you'll stay on the grounds and not go wandering further afield.'

The suggestion was sensible. It shouldn't make her want to rage and rail at him. She gave a single nod.

He pushed her phone at her. 'And ring me if you find yourself bamboozled or lost. Promise me.'

She pulled in a breath. 'I promise.'

She didn't know for how long she wandered. One thing became clear, though. She sure as heck wasn't enjoying the beauty of the landscape as it turned into the kind of winter wonderland she'd only read about in fairy tales.

And it deserved to be enjoyed!

She jumped up and down on the spot in sudden fury, grateful no one was nearby to witness her temper tantrum, but she needed to rid her body of the panic and anger that gripped it. She succeeded eventually by trudging so hard and so fast repeatedly around the orchard that instead of wanting to hit something, she wanted to cry.

Why did Beau have to go and ruin everything?

Fashioning snow into a ball, she hurled it at the trunk of a tree. And missed.

It had been such a perfect day until he'd gone and ruined it. She thought back to their present opening beside the Christmas tree, her family's high spirits, the fire in the hearth... Brushing snow from the stile, she planted herself on it, chin in hands, wishing she could scrub the memory from her mind as easily.

The presents he'd given her... The jumper had been Christmas fun, pure and simple, but the darts and the recipe book were perfect. *So perfect.* Because of the memories they'd made since she'd arrived here, the in jokes they'd developed. They'd *meant* something.

Her shoulders slumped. She didn't want to lose Beau's friendship. It was the last thing she wanted to do.

Her fingers stole to the fine chain at her throat. The necklace he'd given her was the most beautiful thing she'd ever seen. She was creating a garden for him and he'd given her one to take with her wherever she went. It was beautiful, filled with meaning and—she swallowed—romantic.

But she didn't want romance.

Look inside your own heart.

She shot to her feet. Damn it, Beau Diamond had no idea what was in her heart.

She set to pacing again. The urge to weep and

wail, to throw things and yell at the top of her voice, gripped her in waves.

Eventually she slammed to a halt.

Oh, for heaven's sake, get over it. So what if the man loves you? You were upfront. You didn't lie. He'll get over it.

Except... She swallowed. It wasn't fair. Beau didn't deserve a broken heart. He'd been so kind to her—grumpy and blustery when she'd needed him to be, but generous too. And he'd challenged her in ways that no one else had. In ways that had made her start to see the future in a very different light. She owed him so much.

And now that he had finally reclaimed the dreams he'd thought were dust, he deserved to go into that future with a heart full of hope.

Her lip curled. 'While we're on the subject, Chlo, why haven't you been over the moon about his new contract when it's what he wanted and what you urged him to fight for?' Because that *did* deserve some serious soul-searching.

Because he'll forget all about his secret garden.

'No way,' she breathed. 'I am not that petty and small-minded.'

Because he'll forget all about you.

Her hands clenched. 'But that's what I want!'

Somewhere inside her, her secret hidden self raised a fierce eyebrow. *Really?*

Her mind whirled. Beau's presents might've been perfect, but her presents to him had been equally perfect. *Perfect.* It occurred to her then how often she'd used that word today and her mouth dried.

This Christmas had been perfect, not because they'd managed to put on a damn fine show for her family, but because she'd spent the day with him. She and Beau had created all the trappings of a perfect Christmas and thrown themselves into it wholeheartedly.

She just hadn't wanted to acknowledge how wholeheartedly.

Because the feelings she'd developed for Beau were deep and strong and lasting, and that terrified her. It had sent her running like a champion sprinter.

As if she could outrun a broken heart!

Her heart thumped and she had to brace herself against an apple tree. If she walked away from Beau now she wouldn't just be breaking his heart, she'd be breaking her own too.

She loved him. She loved his sense of humour, she loved the way he laughed, and she loved his passion for the natural world. She loved his kindness, his wisdom and the way he touched her. She loved his courage. She loved *him*.

But if he should die in two years' time, leaving her alone and the life they'd built together shattered... She covered her face with a groan. Oh, God, that would be harder than walking away now. So much harder.

If you had your time again, would you walk away from Mark to spare yourself the heartbreak?

The breath jammed in her chest. Would she?

Very slowly she shook her head. *No.*

So was she going to live a half-life now, protecting her heart and keeping it safe? Or was she going to find the courage to choose perfection with no guarantees?

Their life together might only last a year or two. *But it might last a lifetime.*

She was barely aware of turning, but she found herself running towards the house as fast as she could, shouting Beau's name at the top of her voice.

He burst from the house and pelted towards her. 'What's wrong?' He grabbed her by the upper arms and scanned the surroundings. 'What spooked you?'

'Me,' she wheezed, gripping his forearms and bending to try and get air into burning lungs. 'So unfit,' she wheezed, straightening.

'It's the cold, makes it hard to catch your breath.' He frowned. 'And what do you mean you spooked yourself?'

'Love.' She released him to press her hands into the small of her back and drag in as measured a breath as she could, tried to slow the crazy racing of her heart. 'Love spooked me.'

One eyebrow lifted. 'Like that's news.'

She folded her arms and glared back. 'You

snuck up on me. You weren't supposed to be so damn perfect. You sure as hell weren't supposed to be so hot! I didn't want to feel things again, but you made me feel things anyway.'

'So? You made me feel things too. While calling me an idiot, I might add. Only seems fair to me.'

'Oh, really?' She poked a finger to the delicious hardness of his chest. 'You think love's fair, do you?'

He stilled.

'I didn't want to fall in love with you, Beau Diamond!' Was she yelling?

He stilled.

'I've been trying to hide from that truth, using every means at my disposal, and then you just oh-so-casually tell me you love me and want more, and—' she hitched up her chin '—you have to know that's going to spook a girl like me. I mean, how are we even going to work? We live on different sides of the globe, and you're going to be flitting here and there all over the world filming your new series. When would we even see each other?'

His face gentled. 'Chloe—'

'Don't you dare interrupt me!' She pointed a finger at him, but her vision had blurred, and she had to blink hard to bring him back into focus. 'I love you, Beau.'

He smiled down at her, those blue eyes so true and knowing. 'I love you too, Chloe.'

She had to fight the answering smile building through her too. She shrugged, aiming for casual. 'I know, you already said.' That delicious grin of his widened and it took an effort not to get all caught up in it, to just kiss him now and save the hard questions for later.

She sobered and straightened. *Be brave.*

'You said you wanted more. How much more do you want? Because I have to warn you I want it all—lifetime commitment, children...the works.'

'Then we're on the same page.' He swept her up in his arms and kissed her so soundly and thoroughly that if any doubts had remained they'd have dissolved beneath the fierceness of his lips. Lifting his head, he stared down at her, and the possessiveness in his eyes made her soul sing. This man was hers. And she was his.

'Right, then.' She hiccupped, and tried to get her rampaging pulse under control. 'You're going to have to promise to be really careful around big cats, and alligators and hippos and any other dangerous animals you're going to be filming from now on.' She couldn't ask him to walk away from his job—it was his passion and he was brilliant at it—but minimising risk wasn't too much to ask.

He smiled down at her, his eyes gentle. 'I've no intention of putting myself at risk, sweetheart.'

The endearment turned her insides to mush.

'And there's something I haven't told you yet about my new series. I've no intention of traipsing to the far-flung corners of the world any more.'

She blinked.

'Being back here at Dawncarden, discussing the garden and the pipistrelles with you, has given me a brand-new direction. I want to show people—*real people*—what we have here right on our doorstep. I want to show them how they can nurture wildlife in their own gardens. I want to inspire them to at least try.'

She had every confidence he would too. 'That sounds wonderful.'

'I've been given the go-ahead by the powers that be, and we're going to start filming in three months.'

Hope stirred. And excitement. 'Are you saying you're going to be based here at Dawncarden?'

'That's exactly what I'm saying.' He grinned. 'And I was thinking that if you happened to find yourself offered contracts to makeover gardens on grand estates here in the UK, maybe I could convince you to make Dawncarden your base too.'

That sounded *perfect*.

A short time later she found herself sitting in his lap on the sofa in front of the roaring fire, Rudy curled up in his basket nearby making cute little puppy noises as he dreamed. 'I was an idiot for blurting out that I loved you the way that I did, Chloe. I'm sorry, I knew you needed more time.'

'Well, if I hadn't tried to get you into bed, you wouldn't have needed to tell me you wanted more than just sex.'

'You have no idea how tempted I was to take you up on the offer and to hell with the consequences.'

She rested a hand against his cheek. 'No, you deserved more, and you were right to demand it. You should never short-change yourself, Beau. *Never*.'

His finger trailed a path down her cheek to her collarbone, those perfect lips lifting. 'It was you who taught me not to settle for something less.'

Her?

'You made me realise that in shutting myself away all I was doing was hurting myself. Some people aren't worth my trust, but they're also not worth me burying myself for either. You made me see there are people in the world who can see behind the scars and gossip. You taught me to fight for what I want. If you hadn't come to Dawncarden, I'd have still been here in fifty years' time, a bitter and angry recluse.'

She shook her head. 'You'd have found your feet again. I'm sure of it. You were ready for a push, that's all. And we both know I'm the pushy sort so clearly it was a match made in heaven.'

He kissed her, and she kissed him back with everything she had—all her joy and gratitude and love.

He lifted his head, breathing hard. 'What made you decide to take the risk on us?'

She glanced down at her hands. 'Losing Mark was… It was awful.'

A finger beneath her chin lifted her gaze back to his. 'I know you loved Mark. There's no need to feel awkward about that. I'm not jealous. I'm sorry he died, and I'm sorry you had to go through so much grief and heartache.'

The warmth in his smile eased the burn at the centre of her, and she nestled against him more firmly. 'Clearly—' she rolled her eyes '—I never expected to find another man who could be so perfect for me, but I think I fell in love with you from the very first moment you snarled at me. Crazy, right? But I just felt so free to be me again. It was such a relief, Beau. I just didn't recognise then what it was or what it meant.' They'd both been on such a journey during the last six weeks.

'When I was stomping around your orchard in the snow just then I realised that, even given all the pain losing Mark caused, I would never give up the time we'd had together.'

She placed her hand over his heart. 'And then I realised that I'd be a fool to walk away from you and the life we could have, just because one day I might lose it. Nothing else in this world could make me happier than you, Beau. *Nothing.* So, in the end, although it took me far too long to work it out, it was a no-brainer.'

His fingers trailed across her cheek. 'You are the most amazing woman I've ever met—beautiful, brave, smart. I'm going to cherish your heart, and I'm going to make you feel blessed every single day.'

'And will you promise to still snarl at me when you feel snarly?'

'I will if you will.'

She crossed her heart. 'And will you promise to keep kissing me every single day as if it's your favourite thing to do?'

He grinned. 'That's easy to promise. It *is* my favourite thing to do.'

'And will you promise to keep sampling my attempts at shortbread?'

He threw his head back and laughed. 'Now that's going above and beyond, but I promise.'

And then he kissed her, and they didn't speak again for a very long time.

EPILOGUE

Two and a half years later

'TA-DA!'

Chloe blinked when Beau whipped off the scarf he'd used to cover her eyes. She stared at the scene in front of them and her heart expanded until she thought she might float right up into the sky.

Beau had set a table with the same French champagne and selection of delicacies that they'd had for their wedding twelve months ago. Not only that, he'd decorated their secret garden with ribbons and bunting and fairy lights, just as it had been on their wedding day.

She clasped her hands beneath her chin. 'Oh, Beau, how did you manage to do all of this without me knowing?'

He shrugged, and his mouth hooked up in one of *those* grins, making her pulse flutter. He must've been up with the larks. Speaking of which, they had a nesting pair in the near corner and every day she expected to hear the sound of baby birds cheeping.

He popped the champagne. 'Happy anniversary, Chloe.' He raised his glass. 'To the most wonderful woman I've ever met. The last two and a half years have been the happiest I've ever known.'

She touched her glass to his. 'To the most wonderful husband a woman could ever have.' She took the tiniest of sips, glancing around again, remembering the scene here a year ago.

Beau had flown all of her family and friends to the UK. Beau's grandmother and Chloe's immediate family had stayed at Dawncarden, while extended family members and friends had been put up at The Nag's Head and various bed and breakfasts in Ballingsmallard. Mark's family included. They'd been so happy for her. The whole village had been buzzing and, of course, had turned out for the wedding too.

They'd had a simple service here in the walled garden, with a festive buffet lunch afterwards, overseen by Stephanie, in the orchard. Long tables that had been set beneath the fruit trees, and a local band had played. It had been a meal filled with love and laughter and more joy than Chloe had ever thought possible. The day had been *perfect*.

'Happy?' he murmured, entwining his fingers with hers and strolling along one of the paths, the garden lush and green and gorgeous all around them.

She squeezed his hand. 'More than I ever thought possible.'

He pressed a kiss to her knuckles. 'In a small

way, I wanted to recreate our wedding day. Marrying you, Chloe, was the happiest day of my life.'

'Better than getting the news that your new series had topped the ratings?' she teased.

'Even better than that,' he said, but his shoulders went back. 'That was a pretty good day too, though.'

She'd been thrilled for him. He'd worked so hard to make the series not just interesting and informative but enthralling. She didn't know how he did it. And she wasn't the only one impressed. The fan mail he received blew her away. He was having such an influence on what people now wanted to achieve with their gardens and the wild places in their neighbourhoods.

'I'm not the only one who's gone from strength to strength.' His hand tightened about hers. 'Have you decided which contract you're going to accept next?'

In the last two years, she'd transformed not one, but three gardens on grand estates—one in Dorset, another in Cheshire and the last in Norfolk—as well as working on a public park in Birmingham. Though she and Beau did their best to align their schedules, there were the inevitable absences. It was the only shadow in an otherwise sunny existence, and as they both loved their work it was hard to begrudge it.

As all of the gardens she'd worked on had been high profile, receiving a lot of publicity, she was now in high demand in her own right. She'd recently been asked to create a knot garden at a royal estate, to transform the grand gardens of a Kensington mansion, while the Australian Botanical Society had asked her to provide a series of online guest lectures for their members. It all seemed to have happened so quickly. Never in her wildest dreams had she expected such success.

She smiled to herself. She was going to have to slow down a little soon, though. She glanced at Beau. She was waiting to find the perfect moment to share her news with him.

She slipped an arm around his waist. 'I was waiting to find out what your schedule was before making a decision.' It'd be wonderful if they could at least work in the same county for part of the coming months.

They stopped by the hornbeam tree. It was the untidiest corner of the garden, and still their favourite. 'I want to run something past you, Chloe.'

'That sounds ominous.'

'Not ominous. An opportunity. The TV network wants to know if you'd consider filming a segment on each of my shows, giving viewers gardening tips. It'd work brilliantly if we could somehow tie it into the theme of each episode.'

She pulled away, her nerves twanging. 'No way! People don't want to see me. They want to see you.'

'They want to see you too.'

'Not a chance! I—'

'You're chicken, that's what you are.'

Her mouth opened and closed, but she couldn't spit out a single word.

'You're scared of appearing on camera.'

'Happy anniversary, Chloe!' She glared and folded her arms. 'Being on camera is your dream, not mine, and I think one diva in the family is enough, thank you very much.'

'Helping people create wonderful gardens *is* your passion. The series is going from strength to strength. The general public have such a hunger to create their own mini wildlife paradises. *You* can help them do that. Imagine the reach you'd have if you appeared on my show *every week*.'

'Yes but—'

'No buts. This is a great opportunity and you know it.'

Be that as it may, the thought of appearing on TV scared the bejeebies out of her. She'd be tongue-tied and stupid. She'd fumble and mutter and be stupid and—

Gah! She was dying a thousand deaths even thinking about it.

He crossed his arms, his eyes full of challenge. 'Working together means we wouldn't have to spend long periods apart. We'd see each other more, get to spend more time together.'

Which would be perfect, but…

Tongue-tied, fumbling…stupid.

She shuddered.

He bent down to peer into her eyes. 'What are you really afraid of?'

She hitched up her chin and glared. 'I don't know how to talk to camera.'

'You wouldn't be thrown in at the deep end. You'd get training from some of the best in the industry.'

She would? She rolled her shoulders as temptation coiled around her. It would mean spending more time with Beau. She shook herself. 'I'd make mistakes and look stupid on camera, and that'd make me sound like I've no idea what I'm doing or what I'm talking about. I'd lose all credibility.'

'Do I look stupid when I make mistakes?'

She waved that away. 'You don't make mistakes.'

He laughed as if she genuinely amused him and she could feel her eyes narrow. He held up his hands. 'You would have a final say in what went to air. If you don't like something, we cut it.'

She stilled. Her heart started to pound. 'Do you mean that?'

He crossed his heart.

She pointed a finger at him. 'You've pulled strings to make this happen.' Because even through her fear of appearing in public, she could see how perfect this could be.

'I swear I haven't. It was the network head's idea. He's friends with Abercrombie.'

The owner of the garden she'd made over in Norfolk?

'He's done his research, been to have a look at each of the gardens you've worked on. It's why he invited himself to Dawncarden for the weekend last month. He wanted to see how you sounded, how you moved, and if he thought you'd be able to do it.'

Which probably explained the man's somewhat puzzling interest in her plans for Dawncarden's orchard.

'If I'd known what he was up to, I'd have warned you.'

She believed him. They might not always see eye to eye, but they always had each other's back.

He pulled her in for a heated and very thorough kiss. When he eased away she had to brace a hand against his chest and fight the urge to pull his head back down to hers.

'Will you at least think about it?' he asked.

When he looked at her like that she couldn't deny him anything. She pulled in a breath, faced her fear. If there was one thing she'd learned since meeting Beau, it was to not let fear govern her. 'Beau, there's nothing to think about.'

His eyes dimmed, but he reached out and touched her face and found a smile anyway, before taking her hand and starting back along the path. 'Okay.'

'No.' She shook his hand. 'What you're suggesting is *perfect*. I'd be an idiot to turn such an opportunity down.'

He swung back, his face lighting up.

'But you have to promise you won't let me look stupid on camera.'

'I promise.'

His eyes burned into hers with such warmth, she told herself she could deal with a few nerves if it made him happy.

Speaking of happy…

Her heart started to thump. 'It's perfect, not just because it means we'll see more of each other, but I want to start slowing down a little. I need to.' She took his hand and held it against her stomach. 'Beau, we're going to have a baby.'

He stared at her as if he couldn't comprehend what she was telling him. 'A baby?' he parroted, and she found herself suddenly laughing for the sheer joy of it.

'The doctor confirmed it through the week. Both me and baby are doing fine. So that means you need to get to work redecorating the nursery.'

With a whoop, he lifted her up and swung her around. Setting her back on her feet, he smoothed her hair from her face, his eyes shining. 'That's the best news ever.'

Lifting her into his arms, he strode the length of the garden to set her on a chair at the table, his gentleness bringing tears to her eyes. 'You need to rest.'

'Nonsense!' But she let him fuss because it was lovely, and the light in his eyes made her melt… and because she loved him so much.

'You're happy?' he checked, kneeling by her side.

'Over the moon,' she assured him. 'You?'

'So happy.' He cupped her face. 'It's perfect. I feel…' he shook his head, his eyes shining 'blessed.'

She nodded.

'I was blessed the day you came into my life, Chloe *Ivy Belle* Jennings. You made me realise my life could still be full and worthwhile and good.'

She leaned forward and pressed her lips to his. 'You gave me back to myself, Beau, helped me be whole again. And together we're going to create a family that will love and laugh and be strong for each other.'

He kissed both her hands. 'I am going to do everything I can to look after you and the baby, Chloe, and anybody else who comes along. I don't want any of you wanting for anything.'

'Beau, all we want is you.'

Her breath caught at the look in his eyes and her pulse fluttered. She pulled him up to sit in a chair and planted herself in his lap. 'Did you bring a blanket?'

'Of course.'

'And did you lock the garden door behind us?'

He nodded, his eyes dancing. 'The key is in my pocket.'

'Then I think it's time you kissed me again.'

'I couldn't think of anything I'd rather do.'

And then he kissed her, as if kissing her was his very favourite thing to do.

* * * * *

If you enjoyed this story, check out these other great reads from Michelle Douglas

Wedding Date in Malaysia
Escape with Her Greek Tycoon
Cinderella and the Brooding Billionaire
Billionaire's Road Trip to Forever

All available now!